REPLENISH

Book 1 in the elemental series

By – N. A. Kimmage

© Copyright 2018

Thank you to all those who kept their faith in me, you guys never gave up on me, even though there were days when I couldn't face dealing with this book.

Firstly to Amelia – my bookworm daughter, thank you.

To Gemma – for giving me that final push, even though it wasn't quite ready, without that push, it wouldn't have made it to publishing.

To Brian, cheers for putting up with me in moments of writer mania.

To everyone else, I cannot thank you all enough. Yes the dedication page is after the title page, I like being different I guess.

My biggest thanks go to my mum and dad, thank you for the passion of reading, without that, I doubt this book would have been written.

A little something from me – Never give up on your dreams. X

CHAPTER 1 – LANDSCAPES AND FARAWAYS

Within this smoke-filled town there is life. Hearts beat like drums and the chatter of people can be heard above the noise of traffic. The concrete beneath their feet is dry, akin to an arid desert.

No-one notices the girl with the pale Gray eyes and the haunted face. She glides in and out of the market only speaking when spoken to. Her ebony hair glistens in the sunlight, like a shard of light from heaven. It isn't that she has nowhere to go, it is something more than that; such are those with broken hearts and burdens upon their shoulders.

Her clothes are plain and simple - a purple satin shirt, black trousers and flat blue shoes. If you ever see her walking by, it might make you think 'Have I seen a ghost?' You'd be half right, for although she is part of the living, her soul is dead, and her spirit lingers in the dark.

Through the winding streets, where in Summer the sun blinds you with its sheer beauty and in Winter snow glistens like a dark, barren landscape scattered with diamonds.

To the West of town, where narrow lanes stretch for miles, wild flowers grow, and woodlands lurch out at you. Beyond that are little streams that trickle, a lake mid-way down the next valley, tractors in the wide open green fields can be heard, cows graze or laze about, sheep look out of place - looking more like fluffy white clouds against the green and yellow fields.

The weather within these two valleys can switch quickly, even during the height of Summer, one minute there is glorious sunshine, the next grey rain clouds appear, and mist descends, well what would you expect? This is Yorkshire after-all.

Here is where heaven lives, truly a magnificent place where dreams can come true and where the hills stretch towards the sky in some eternal dance.

As we make our way back down the narrow country lanes, there is a lonesome house just to the right of the first valley. It basks in rays of sunshine. This is a steadfast house, built to last a lifetime, maybe even more. The weathered sandstone bricks caress dark wood window frames, a simple oak wood front door which I'm told is built to last forever, a diamond window pane finishes off the ageless look.

Within the walls sadness creeps from every pore, once there was happiness, love and hope, now all that remains is loss, guilt and loneliness.

A car drives up the narrow lane and stops metres from the house, out gets the girl with the pale gray eyes and the haunted face. She wanders up to the top of the valley, watching the lake below as it drifts gently with the breeze. She gazes longingly up at the sky, hoping for something that can never happen. She cannot change events, what's done is now done but what kind of future can she have, if she can't let go of the past?

Lonely, she wanders down the valley, back to her home. Once a refuge from the world, now a place of painful memories.

Once inside the house, the girl breaks down in tears, cursing, swearing and hanging on tight to a cream coloured cushion that rests upon a deep coffee coloured sofa. The dark polished wood floor reflects sunlight as it bounces off a mirror above the open fire. Family photos adorn the walls, a large white book case stands in the far corner with a comfy cream chair. A handmade rug lays on the floor, the patterns are of swirls, much like this girls' life - so mixed up and never ending.

Bright sunshine illuminates where she kneels weeping quietly, unable to console herself, she is in free-fall, not knowing where she may one day - land.

Her tears stain the wood floor, her tears are like an endless rain; each tear is unique and each one in torment. Only her eyes show a tiny spark of life, her life could at one time rival the sun.

No-one sees the pain and sorrow she hides, trying to believe that good still exists in the world that – in her own mind, is against her.

She's never been on a date, never kissed someone, had someone to hold her and whisper in her ear that everything will be fine, that one day things will change.

Her heart beats like any other human, it is broken, never really repairing itself, a piece is missing which will never return.

The warmth she once radiated could light anyone's way in the dark, the tenacity stirs constantly from within, but the darkness overshadows her, she's lost in the dark, unable to find the light.

It is time for her to stand up and take heed to the person she will one day become, that is when she no longer feels lost and afraid to stand alone in the dark.

Chapter 2 – Free-fall

Late for work again, slamming into the bedroom door then dashing into the bathroom with my sore nose to quickly brush my teeth, afterwards put clothes on and straight out the front door, only to realise this is my week off, 'Damn it,' I growl still with the keys in the car door. With my shoulders slouched I drag my body back in the house and flop on the sofa.
I work in a boring office, where everyone is a robot and we take orders from a couch potato of a boss who sits on his throne like a God.

When you haven't much to do, your mind tends to wander. Mine is taking me on a trip I'd long since forgotten. It was Winter, the open fire was full of logs that crackled away, a roast in the oven, making the senses fizz with delight: Mum is tending to the veg in the boiling pan, in the corner was a little girl reading a book aloud and Dad sitting in his favourite rocking chair. The scene changes quickly into one of devastation and fear.

Reality bites, a warm inviting house with lovely memories, yet laced with bitter, sour memories of the recent past, the past that had consumed me, leaving me weak.

Stepping into the kitchen a floorboard in the room creaks softly as a gentle breeze comes drifting by, taking a deep breath I half smile, tears fall from my half open eyes.

A few hours have passed, it's only 11.00am, my head is stuck in a book about Mythical creatures, dreaming of the adventures I could have, only in my dreams mind but it was a way to escape my grim reality, the magnificent dragons even the demonic dogs held my attention, but the majestic Phoenix really captures and holds me in all its glory.

Did they ever exist? These creatures of Myth? Did they lurk beneath the surface of the mortal realm? For a time when they could rise again and rule the world. Or maybe they were already amongst us? Plain as day but due to our inability to see beyond the norm we were blind, which made it easier for them to move about our mortal world? Watching us make a mess of things and bring cruelty and devastation upon it?

A knock on the door brought me out of my daze, 'Hi.' I smile at my local postman, 'How's you?'

'Am not bad ta,' He replies as he hands me my mail, 'Bit nippy out 'ere though.' He rubs his arms.

'Storm comin'' I'd say, ya best get ya rounds done before it hits, feels like it's gonna be a big one.' Smelling the air again, the storm isn't far from arriving.

'How d'you know that?' He enquires.

'Jus' sommat in the air, a change in temperature or electrical interference, catch ya again and remember be careful.' I wave as he walks away, he waves just before disappearing out of sight.

Soon as I shut the door, tears came streaming down my face, I could not control my emotions like I could everything else, this was outside my capacity.

If tears were steps; I could step all the way to the moon with the amount I have shed.

At work I was fine, there was little worry of me crying, but after work, driving home it would build until I could no longer contain it, 'Shadows on those who cry too much, have fallen through wars and never felt the love.' It was a quote from one of my all-time favourite books – Longing by S. Morris. I had been loved, now it had left me.

I need to release some of this pain, maybe a walk up the valley and maybe even some practice with my sword (for my fencing lessons I'd been neglecting over the past three weeks,) that might help? The clouds are gathering, though I doubt the storm is ready yet.

The clouds roll away and the sun re-appears as I step out, running inside I drop my sword off and decide to take a walk instead to one of my favourite childhood haunts – the field next to the woods.

Touching the tree just on the outer edge of the woods, my fingers trace the mark I left so many years ago – my initials, it is my all-time favourite tree, it was slightly taller than the rest, some low gnarled branches which in summer birds would use as a look out on an evening, right now it looked as if it was reaching for something that was out of reach, maybe it wanted to touch the sky and curl its branches around the stars.

I stand there wishing things would change, suddenly, the dark clouds appear and before I'm able to move rain pours down like sheets, thunder rumbles above and lightning streaks across the sky like an angry god.

My vision blurs, fire burns through my veins and before I knew it, I'm running faster than any normal human could ever run. Somehow, I feel free, my eyes take in every small detail of the valley; the way the lightning hits the ground for split second and lights up the woods to the West – the woods I had just left.

In a short space of time I'm back where I started, still I'm in shock, not knowing if I had just imagined what had happened, but that was not possible, it was real and whatever the case, wasn't part of my imagination. The fire in my veins vanished, leaving me wondering exactly what had just occurred, I had no explanation, nor did I have anyone I could ask for advice.

The storm rumbled above me, I was soaked to the bone, still I felt there was something different about myself. Walking at a steady pace, I walk back down towards my house, listening to the Gods or Goddesses of the sky battle it out.

Chapter 3 - Flashes and Visions

It had been happening more and more often – flashes of things I had never seen before. I went through a phase aged thirteen but had dismissed it as wild imagination.

Visions of fires, horses, battles and a dragon. The first flashback happened after work a few months ago, I'd started the engine when it occurred – I was on horseback riding at full speed towards something that I felt would be my last view of the world, riding alone, it felt as if I was on a mission, the landscape felt fresh, surrounded by hills and forts. Must have been late spring or early Summer. After a moment it faded, leaving me shaking and confused.

Even in my dreams I could not escape these feelings. For the past few days nothing had happened, I wonder if the whole flashbacks and visions had been real?

I needed to break away from here, to escape and go somewhere for the day, I needed – release.

So here I find myself in Leeds, about fifteen miles South-West of where I live. The hustle and bustle really isn't my scene, but I go for a coffee anyway, before heading towards the moorland above Bradford.

Exactly what is required - a picnic high on the hills over-looking Bradford and beyond. Laying down on the blanket I stare at the light blue sky.

In that moment it feels as if the ground is shaking, but it can't be, we don't get Earthquakes like this in England? Do we?

Whatever just happened, vanished as suddenly as it had appeared, 'I need to go home, this day is too strange!'

There had been an accident on the motorway, I knew a short cut home and turn the car around ready to take the back roads home.

For some unknown reason I had to pull over, get out and run towards the field near the foot of a hill.

I stretch out my arms, not knowing why and then - whoosh! Things begin to change, though the hill stays the same. A few yards away from me I see a girl no older than sixteen with a sword, she sticks it into the ground and sits down. My eyes watch her curiously, warily. Another figure emerges, his eyes are pale blue, his hair like sunshine, his body muscular and his top half bare. He wraps his arms around her and for a moment she cradles him before standing up and for the first time, she speaks, 'It is almost time.'

Within me - feelings of excitement and fear stirred.

Suddenly, I wasn't me anymore, looking at who I had become, I was the female I had been watching. There were voices calling different names and I responded when someone called 'Isla.'

I go with the flow. The figures in the distance were now no more than two feet away from me, I'd ran to them after they called my name, then something odd occurred; One minute I was human, when I next glimpse there was a dragon in my place. I was being pulled further into this vision and I had no choice but to follow.

Up Into the air the dragon climbed and with such immense speed it took my breath away.

Higher and higher I went, as I scanned the ground below I could make out lots of little fires and people sitting around them. The person that had called my name earlier seemed to run with such speed, surely that wasn't human? I then realised he was on horseback and I was slowing down. The others weren't far behind.

Somehow the male that had called my name was now communicating with me via telepathy. 'Head due North Isla, stay safe and remember you mean the world to me.'

The voice echoed in my mind, a warm feeling now replaced the feeling of excitement.

It was then I replied, 'Thank you, you mean so much to me too, I am ready, and you only say that because we head for the battle line.' I feel myself smile.

Going into battle? With what? What was the point of asking these questions? I'd shortly find out the answer. Sure enough a few moments later all my questions were answered.

About five-hundred yards ahead I could make out line after line of advancing troops, they weren't in uniform, they were in normal dress. Something about them made me shiver. I dived sharply, landing a hundred yards from where the lines had halted behind me, the male was already there flanked by the others. I noticed their skin had a weathered look, who were these people? Whoever they were I was drawn to them, like we had some unbreakable bond.

My eyes then focused on the advancing troops, who stopped 120yrds from where we were stood. All of them had a different skin tone to my companions, their skin was deathly pale, much too pale to be human. There was something different about the troops in front of us; something about their eyes made me shiver. Yes, their eyes, there was nothing but anger pulsing through them.

How were we supposed to defeat them?

An idea came to me; my friends weren't going to go into battle, I wouldn't allow them, it would be only me and me alone. I turned to look at the male that had called my name. I used telepathy to communicate, 'Look Jon, you cannot fight, whatever they are, they are here for me. This I feel is my job, it is what I was designed for. You must go back and warn the others in case I fail. It is my time now, they don't know what to make of me, I'm new to them, they seem scared hahahahaha.' I couldn't hide the fury and excitement in my voice.

There was an edge of panic to his voice 'What are you saying? You're mad!' Sadness crept into his response 'I know you were designed for this, but it doesn't have to be this way.' His tone changed to that of longing and desolation, 'I'll send the others back to get reinforcements, I'm fighting alongside you, I will not leave you.'

'When are you going to learn to let go of me Jon? I know I love you, a true bond that cannot be broken. I have to dismiss those feelings, the call to protect is far stronger, when time calls for us to fight once again I will see you, maybe not in the form you are now, but in some other form and known by a different name and maybe even be one of them, you will not be like them in that way, with their red eyes and burning fury. Please do as I say.' There was pleading both in my voice and my eyes.

One of the females turned towards me and spoke aloud 'You are right Isla, so right, we will all be together again, different looks, voices and memories but we will find one another.' She turned to Jon and said, 'You know you must do as she says, reinforcements are what we need, she will be okay on her own for a while.'

Jon sighed heavily, he knew she was right. He signalled to the rest to retreat, they all raced off into the distance. I had one last thought to give them all 'Thank you for being here for me. Now it is time to rise from the ashes of a dying world.'

The female replied, 'It was our honour to serve as your protectors.'

A moment later they were out of sight. It was now me and these troops, staring each other down.

Soon the fight would commence, they were waiting for the signal. I could feel my instincts kicking in, I knew they were ready, I decided to pre-empt and attack first.

Flying at the lines of troops, I roared and tore my way through them, ripping at least twenty of them apart, then setting them on fire. There was a screeching sound as I ripped them apart and the agonizing screams of the wretched creatures.

A sudden sharp pain hit me on the side of the head, like a thousand darts, the pain was like nothing I had ever felt before, still I continued onwards.

Time seemed to accelerate, and I found myself lying on top of a steep banking, crying out in agony.

As I looked to one side I could see bodies of the warriors that my companions had gone back to get. Turning to my other side, I could see Jon and the remaining survivors surrounding me. I looked down at myself, to see that I was back to my human self, I had no clothes on. Blood covered and matted my hair. Pain pierced my lungs and I wanted to scream; but that would only hurt me more. At the same time, I knew we had been victorious. I knew I was dying, I didn't feel hopeless, pain consumed my body.

Jon was stroking my head and soothing me, 'Please stay.' He begged.

I spat out the words with blood hitting Jon's face, 'The battle has been won Jon, be glad of that. My time is almost up death draws near.' Taking a deep breath that pierced my lungs, 'Do not be sad, any of you, I have served my purpose, be happy that the war is won. The phoenix rises from the ashes of death, disaster and anything that gets in the way. I will be watching; my time will come again and that will be the last time.' I managed to smile crookedly.

There were tears streaming down everyone's face. With my last gurgling scream, I was drowning in my own blood, it was at this point my eyes closed.

My eyes opened to familiar surroundings: the tears streaming down my cheeks. I was dazed as I stood by the hill, slowly but surely, I made my way back to the car.

After an hour and a half, I was back home. Questions raced through my mind and I knew from deep within no-one could answer them or help me find out what was happening.

Chapter 4 - The Stranger

Sunlight floods my bedroom as I sit watching early morning television. I get sick of people moaning about their lives, they should walk a mile in someone else's shoes, someone who is far removed from their world.

Turning the television off I wonder about my visions - were they real? Or just imagination? It felt as if only I held the answers; buried somewhere in my soul.

I wanted adventure, I wanted love and most of all I desired to be part of a loving family, since my own were no longer here.

My visions were of battles long since passed, each ended the same way - victory and death. I had noticed two things - the dragon and all its power, the passion and fire it exuded and my incident; being able to run at immense pace, far faster than any human, there had to be a connection between these events.

Walking into the kitchen I could still see the visions in my mind, feelings of something I hadn't felt for a long time - feelings of belonging, of purpose, feelings of devotion and calling.

Sitting down on the creaky kitchen chair I quickly down my drink of tea, grab my sword and walk out of the front door, intent on practising. The breeze was brisk, but the sun was warm and soothing. Hardly any traffic came by as I wandered further up towards the moors stretching before me.

The sword sliced through the air, it was as if I had always meant to wield such a weapon.

Only low-pitched sounds emitted by the sword were heard as it sliced through the air. In the blink of an eye it looked like someone had pressed the fast-forward button on a remote, the sword and my arms were getting quicker. My eyes followed the movements as if I was simply practising at normal speed. Something made me stop suddenly; looking over my shoulder, a shadow emerges from the woods three miles away.

'Why is it I can see so far away?' I question myself.

My heart starts to beat faster as the shadow draws ever closer.

I dare not look, my fingers lock around my sword with an iron grip, the fire rises within and I'm scared as to what might happen.

Taking one last look, glancing across; it is a man with cropped silver hair, he stops feet from where I'm stood and bows his head, the fear in me subsides, although the fire in me keeps on rising.

I bow my head in return, as I look up his outline shimmers and fades, the next second I am looking into the eyes of a silver-grey wolf. The wolf is much bigger than a normal sized wolf, I have to crane my neck, I look into his peaceful eyes. Looking towards the ground, his shadow is still human,

'What the hell is going on?' I ask myself.

My mind swirls with possibilities, when I look at the stranger, he is once again human. I'm stood there wondering why he hasn't spoken.

'Hi,' I say with my lips quivering, 'I'm Lydia.' I feel such an idiot, to my surprise the stranger replies.

'Greetings dear Lydia,' He continues in his American accent, 'My name is Daniel and you don't know how long we have been searching for you.' He sounded relieved.

Instantly I'm babbling, almost incompetently, 'What? Am I being head hunted? Can someone please,' I take a deep breath, 'tell me what the fuck is going on? My life is confusing as is, but this is a whole new ball game.' I plunge the sword deep into the ground, sit down and breathe in and out slowly. My head swims with too many things. Grabbing my bag, I dig out a cigarette and lighter, 'I only smoke when stressed.'

I hadn't touched a cigarette in two years. I allow the smoke to touch the back of my throat before releasing it into the air.

Daniel sits down beside me and starts talking, 'As you can probably tell by my accent, I'm from America, I grew up in Maine-' He stops himself, after a tense moment of silence he talks softly, 'You probably have many questions, some of which I can answer, as for the rest, that is for you to answer.'

He looks deep into my eyes, his reaction scares me, Daniel backs up slightly.

I extinguish the cigarette. My fingers start trembling with fear, I try and keep my voice even and calm, 'Something wrong?'

His face registers shock, his eyes, however they also register a kind of understanding, 'So much pain, so much confusion, so much loss and so much fear, you've held it all back for so long it no longer seems you feel anything anymore; Lydia I know different,' standing up he extends his hand and helps me up, 'You need to calm down, I see your house isn't far away,' he points to the valley below, 'let's head for home, then you can calm down and ask me questions.'

Daniel holds me by the waist, I feel some kind of spark, almost like lightning coursing through me, instead of protesting that it isn't good to talk to strangers despite my age, a feeling from deep within suggests this person, standing facing me has some connection with my soul.

'Hope ya like tea?' What the hell am I saying? 'I also have coffee, if you prefer?' Both sound like a pathetic chat up line.

As we head off back down the moors, Daniel chuckles, 'Either sounds good to me, hope you have cakes and sweets too?'

I smile involuntarily and instead of talking I simply nod my head.

Being back home makes me feel more relaxed, I place my sword down and make Daniel a drink, making sure to bring in the sweets and cakes.

'So, what do you do for a living?' Daniel asks, his mouth full of midget gems.

Sighing and laughing I reply, 'I work in a dull office,' sitting down for a moment I realise, 'I best go have a shower, I'll try not to be long, make yourself at home.'

I head upstairs leaving Daniel happily stuffing his face.

As the shower releases its hot soothing liquid I let myself melt away, letting the hot liquid run down my body and go down the plug hole.

A strange raging fire starts to coarse through my veins; pinning me to the tiled wall, it felt like a volcano - full of rage and resentment, it continued to surge through my veins like lava. My heart beat furiously against my chest and my mind swam with the colour red, it was all I could see. I heard Daniel knocking furiously at the door begging me to let him in.

All I could think was 'Don't break the door.'

Slumped in the bath with the shower still running, I felt the fire retreat and sensation returned to my limbs. Daniel was still knocking on the door, 'Lydia,' He pleads urgently, 'please let me in.'

I answered, my voice shivered 'But I'm naked, go down and wait, I won't be long, I promise.'

Before retreating downstairs Daniel whispers, 'The others will be here soon.' His footsteps fade away.

By early next morning; Daniel and I are still talking away, mainly firing questions at one another, some pleasant, others not so pleasant, at least I have someone who I can fire questions at.

'So, when are the others due'?' I ask whilst making a fry-up, in the kitchen.

'A couple of days,' Daniel changes subject, 'Aw man, you're making me hungry, smells delicious, see my belly is rumblin.' He grins widely.

Listening closely, it does sound as if his stomach is rumbling, but in truth: it is distant thunder, 'Nearly done.' I chuckle as the eggs sizzle away.

I feel comfortable around him, it is like magic. As we eat and drink, the rumbles of thunder creep ever closer. Daniel shows me half chewed food in his mouth, pop flies onto the floor from my mouth as I burst out laughing.

Chapter 5 - The Others

It had been two days since Daniel had arrived, we laughed, we joked, I cried, he offered support, I cooked, and he ate like a pig.

Today there seemed to be tension in the air, thinking aloud I mutter 'Who are the others? Are they like you?'

He squirms in the chair before answering, 'The others are like me in the sense that they've been trying to find you for a long time now, all I can say is they are not like me in other respects, trust me when I say we are here for a specific reason and so are you.' Daniel stands up and looks me straight in the eye.

'You mean all those visions I've been having are for a reason? That seeing myself die in each battle is for a reason?' My voice begins to shake, 'They replay in my mind over and over again, the horror, the pain I feel and the sense of being here before is all for a reason?' I quickly sit down; my legs tremble as does my body.

Daniels eyes open wide with shock, 'You've had visions?'

I nod my head, though I dare not speak.

'How long ago did they start?' He sits on the arm of the chair.

'They began when I was thirteen, it happened for about a year, then they ceased. They began again maybe four or five months ago, yet long enough to make me feel I was going insane, at least now they were not a complete waste.' The sullen tone of my voice lets Daniel know I don't wish to carry on this line of conversation, 'When will they arrive?'

'Not until later.' Smiling a little.

Afterwards we sat in silence, the only sound is the kitchen clock, counting down the seconds and minutes.

It was late afternoon, grey clouds slowly drifted in, covering the glorious sun.

Elsewhere Daniel is taking a nap on the sofa and I was content reading a book curled up on the large sofa, 'Feeling better?' I ask as Daniel wakes up.

Daniel pops his head up from the sofa, followed by his body, 'Loads better thanks,' He looks out of the window, 'Wow, the weather here does change quick.' He chuckles, 'almost time to meet the others, they're excited.' He smiles sincerely.

In an instant I'm out the front door lighting a cigarette, 'Let me finish this then off we go.' I feel like a nervous wreck.

We wander gently up the hill, at the top we dip down the other side slightly and turn to the left. In front of me I spy woodland, 'So this is where we meet the others.' I think to myself, 'Odd place to meet, not much light coming through due to the cloud coverage.' Lots of different thoughts run through my mind.

Out of the shadows two figures emerge, for no reason I start to shiver, a feeling of fear rushes through me, my intake of breath quickens.

As the figures approach, my heart beats at such speed, I wonder if it will beat out of my chest?

One of them has inquisitive eyes of a rich gold, with dark hair, he is well built and has the bone structure to match. The other is taller, younger looking with piercing burnt gold eyes and below his shirt rippled muscles can be seen.

The older of the two steps forward and smiles, 'Hello Lydia.'

'Hi.' I squeak, how embarrassing!

'My name is Michael,' He points at the taller younger guy with him, 'and this is my son - Gabriel,' He turns away before turning back to face me, 'we have been scouring the Earth for you.'

This information shocks me, my mind starts to spin wildly. After a few seconds I'm ready to respond, 'M-m-me?' I can't help but stammer, 'b-but me, there's nothing special about me, are you sure it's me you've been waiting for?'

Michael extends his hand and cups my hand in his, 'You are the one. This news may come as a shock, holding your hand right now, I know you are the one we have been searching for.'

He lets go of my hand, yet my mind still spins and so many questions that need answering. Gabriel's stare brings me back to Earth, 'Yes.' I enquire and shift uneasily.

'Nothing much.' He answers nonchalantly as if I were a child.

Anger boils within my veins, my voice is tainted with dismay and sarcasm, 'I ain't a child you know, I'm old enough to drive, to drink and to know when you're being condescending,' I take a deep breath, 'you don't know me and yet you are judging me.' My arms fold and my expression becomes vacant.

Silence pervades the atmosphere, Michael is first to break it, 'Are you okay dear Lydia?'

Sitting on a branch I take a deep breath, 'I think so,' Looking over at Gabriel, he still has the same look he wore a few moments ago, 'Okay, what's your problem with me?' I stare long and hard at him.

Gabriel comes to within a few feet of me and answers, 'My problem is you, why did we have to search far and wide, you're nothing special,' He sneers, 'well you don't look it, you are what you are; plain, simple and-'

Daniel cuts in, 'That's enough Gabe.' He puts his hand on Gabriel's shoulder.

Back on the ground I scream, 'That's right, plain and simple, that's me, nothing new,' walking backwards I continue to shout, 'why bother? I'm just a waste of time.' I turn and run, not daring to look back.

The next second; I'm in the air, above the trees and I feel exhilarated.

Chapter 6 - Dilemma

'Oh God, am gonna fall any second.' My mind yells but the fall never comes to fruition.

I continue to fly, ever higher and ever faster. Swooping in lower and closing my eyes, it was a shame I didn't see the huge tree trunk, BANG! Down I spiral, landing hard on the floor, 'Ouch, I'm gonna feel that later.' I made a mental note of the fact I will need cleaning up and tend to the minor injuries sustained. I was desperate to scratch my head, only to realise my arms were a set of red wings flecked with gold. Extending them further I felt in awe. Twisting my head around, I notice that although it is streaked with muck I have a huge plumage of a tail, again flecked with red gold and bright yellow, 'This has to be a dream?' It can't have been a dream, nor my imagination.

High above me, the heavens opened, it came crashing down like bullets, closely followed by streaks of lightning and deep rumbles of thunder.

'Time to find shelter.' Looking ahead (not that I could see much due to the driving rain) there was nothing close by, so it was time to head higher into the tree. With each drop of rain, I was getting ever more soaked, every now and again I would shake off the excess moisture.

For at least an hour as the rain poured, my mind was searching for answers to this predicament. After- all, it was questions that raced through my mind, rather than answers I had desired. Okay there has to be an explanation to this, 'Okay, red wings, body, flecked with yellow and gold, what animal is that?' I started to giggle, 'a parrot?'

No, can't be, the wings extended further than Parrot wings. So what else could it be? For some unknown reason my mind flicked to the book on mythology, mentally flicking through the pages, it occurred to me that there was only one answer, 'Phoenix.' I squawked.

The rain ceased but the storm clouds were swirling above me, 'Nah, it can't be, since the rain's stopped, time to go find somewhere like a lake so I can find out for certain.'

My wings extended I aim for the sky and head North-East towards the lake in the next valley, I didn't want to go too close to home, not yet any way.

Light is beginning to fade as I reached the lake, landing quickly at the water's edge, I lean over to stare at my reflection. Jumping back, I realise I am in the form of the Phoenix, 'No way,' looking again I stare longer, spreading my wings and making sure I wasn't dreaming; I dip my head into the icy waters of the lake. 'Nope, not dreaming, wow.' For once I'm lost for words. Again, the heavens open, the sky darker than before.

Staring at my ever-fading reflection, the rain doesn't bother me, but the thought of going home, somehow does.

Now it is completely dark, the feint sounds of church bells could be heard above the tempest, 'I'm soaked here, maybe it's time to head home,' I would have to wait for the rain to cease long enough for me to get home, 'please, cut me a break.' I beg.

After what feels like an eternity, a break in the downpour gives me the opportunity to head home.

Heading East after the church, I'm not far from home.

As I land, I have a funny feeling of being watched, though I scan the darkness, there is nothing or no-one to be seen.

'Ah hell.' I squawk, 'what do I do now?'

My mind ponders over how to change back to my human self. Despite the pounding rain and the ever-increasing thunder, I stand there thinking.

It was time to concentrate upon my human form, it may help, there again it might not, I have to try, I wanted to be in human form.

Several attempts later, I felt my body shudder and shake. I could feel my arms returning, oh what bliss. Looking at myself I realise - I am naked, 'Aw crap,' quickly looking around I make sure no-one is in sight, 'great, I'm naked, it's dark thankfully, but my clothes are at home.' I'm wondering if I should risk staying here or should I go home?

Out from the darkness a voice calls, 'Lydia.'

It sounds like Daniel, I call out, 'Daniel, is that you?'

'Yes, where are-'

A huge clap of thunder interrupts, shortly followed by a streak of lightning, which happens to illuminate my bare body, for a split second.

'Don't come any closer.' I yell in a blind panic.

'Why?' His voice is getting closer.

'Oh God,' I whisper, 'Just say it,' I say to myself, then shout out to Daniel, 'Because I'm naked.'

I hear him laughing.

'Want me to go back and retrieve some clothes for you?' He is still laughing.

Suppressing a giggle, I holler, 'Yes please.' My entire body starts to shudder, I feel cold and obviously I'm soaked.

'I'll be back in five, find somewhere to shelter, I'll find you.' His voice rumbles.

'Okay, thank you.' I start rubbing my arms to get some warmth back in as I walk towards a large hedge at the far end of the field.

Daniel returns with some clothes, I can see his outline, 'This way.' I call.

He hears my voice and turns in my direction. I'm so cold and tired, not to mention hungry.

'I promise not to look.' Daniel sniggers as he hands me a pile of clothes.

'Ha, ha.' I reply.

Despite my soaked skin I quickly put the clothes on and instantly feel warmer. 'Are you mad with me?'

His arms wrap around me, 'No way, you were angry, you ready to go home?'

I shiver at the thought, 'Suppose so.'

'C'mon then, let's go.' He looks at me and notices how wet and pale I look, even in the darkness, 'are you okay?'

'It's been one of those days.'

With that, we walk the half mile back to my home.

Chapter 7 - Questions and Answers

I was day dreaming about BBQ's and snow when Gabriel jolted me back to reality.

It is early the next morning, I hadn't slept, not a common feature for me, nor would I recommend it.

Daniel races over, picks me up and hugs me so tight, he's choking off my air supply.

'Help,' I croak, 'my air supply.'

Immediately he lets go and smiles, 'Sorry.'

I pat him on the back, 'Nah, it's fine.' Looking around, everyone has their eyes on me, 'What?' I protest innocently, a gut feeling is telling me they want to know what happened and who I really am, 'Before we begin I'm off to get a drink and something to eat, anyone else want a drink?'

'I'm good thanks.' Replies Michael.

Gabriel gazes at me, I shift uneasily towards the kitchen, followed by Gabriel.

'Yes.' I enquire.

'Just trying to suss you out.' His smooth voice replies.

'That's gonna take a long time, I can assure you,' The kettle switches off, 'want a drink?'

'No thank you, I'm fine.' He smiles sweetly.

'I'll have one, three sugars.' Daniel calls from the room.

'You want sweet hot water?' I can't help but laugh.

'Hell no, ha ha ha, I'll have a coffee please, with plenty of milk too.'

'Okay.' I sigh getting my breathing back into sync.

Taking Daniels drink into the room, I settle down in my dad's rocking chair, 'Guess you wanna know what happened?'

All three nod, Daniels nose ends up in his cup and I burst out laughing.

'Right, time to begin I guess,' I don't even know if they are ready for this or not? The time for thinking has come to an end. 'One minute I was on the ground, the next I was in the air,' I let them absorb the information before carrying on, 'I felt free, free from everything.' I carried on with the conversation up to the point of the storm, 'Any questions?'

'How old are you?' Gabriel pipes up as he leans forward in the chair.

Okay that's not the question I was ready for and a little intrusive, maybe he was trying yet again to suss me out, 'Twenty-one, why?'

'Interesting.' His eyes sparkle with delight.

'Any sensible questions?' I sigh!

'Has anything on this scale ever happened to you before?' Michael asks.

'No,' I answer, something makes me tell them all about the visions I'd had over recent times, Daniel already knew.

Standing up, 'There was something, don't know if it counts or even matters-'

'Any information could be vital here, in order to piece things together.' Michael replies with such a warm smile, he instantly puts me at ease as I get comfy in the chair.

'Sometimes it's all clear, other times my mind clouds what I've seen. A battle long ago, maybe four hundred years or more, a battle approaches, one moment I'm a girl of sixteen, the next, I'm a dragon.' I catch my breath and decide a break is in order, 'need a break.' and with that I wander outside.

Gabriel follows me out, 'Why do you drink that alcohol?'

The nosey git, I spin around, 'It's my life,' I stare right at him, 'I'll do as I please, no-one can tell me what to do.'

'Well it is a nasty habit,' He retorts, 'It can kill you.'

'So can crossing a road,' my hands wave all over, 'doesn't matter how you live your life, as long as you did what you wanted to achieve.' With that I walk past him and back indoors.

Sitting on the sofa I get comfy, 'Where were we?'

'You were talking about a battle and being a dragon.' Michael eyes me intently and with interest.

'Ah yes,' I remembered, 'It was huge, soaring above everything and everyone,' I felt a shiver run down my spine, 'someone started communicating with me, a battle occurred, and we won, then I died.' This sent shock waves around my body.

'Who were you fighting?' Gabriel asks in a deep melancholy voice.

Looking at him blankly, 'I don't have a clue, though they were advanced, pale, I mean pale and had such angry red eyes, it was as if they were not of this world, what ya might call supernatural.'

Gabriel looks frozen, as if someone has pressed a pause button, quickly he recovers, 'You're supernatural too.' He laughs.

'Maybe.' I smile back.

'How long ya had these dreams/visions?' Asks Daniel, 'By the way this coffee is great.' He chuckles.

'Well, they began maybe nine weeks ago,' My mind takes me back further, to when I was thirteen, every now and again, (I remembered) I'd have nightmares about battles, it echoed through my mind, 'when I turned thirteen, I used to have dreams about battles, dragons, of love, life and of course death, there has to be a connection.' All of a sudden, I feel tired and drained.

'Carry on with the questions, if you guys have any that is?' I smile, my mind feels numb.

'It's not so much a question, rather it is realisation. For a long time it seems your mind, even your dreams have been trying to prepare you for what may eventually arise.' Michael says solemnly.

I answer in a voice that is both confused and lost, 'Hell knows, all I know is this – my heart still beats, yet it stopped long ago, my mind ticks over, but never fully understands, my eyes see what cannot be seen and my body is tired and weak, full of anger and dread.'

Three faces drop, a single tear from Daniels eye, it rolls down his cheek, I wearily walk towards him and hug him, 'Don't be sad, one day things will change for me.' I try to be as convincing as is humanly possible.

He hugs me like a long-lost brother, the embrace is tender yet strong, 'Things will change.' He whispers in my ear.

'I can but try.' I'm starting to drift off to sleep, standing up!

I wake myself up briefly, 'You can all stay here if you want to? There's plenty of room.'

'Are you sure we won't be disturbing you?' Asks Michael.

'I'm sure.' Still hanging on to Daniel.

'Settled.' He shouts, 'where's the food?' He laughs.

Gabriel gives him a stern look, 'Typical.'

'Sorry, didn't mean to be so loud,' Daniel whispers sarcastically, 'was only having a laugh.'

'She's tired, look at her, poor thing.' Gabriel points out.

Voices whisper in a quiet hush, I feel weightless as I drift gently off to sleep

Chapter 8 - **Fever**

Ah hell, I can't open my eyes, must have an eye infection. After ten minutes of ploughing through the grit, I manage to open them, 'How did I get here?' I ask thin air.

The thin air answers, 'We carried you up.' It was Gabriel's voice.

'Oh,' still half dazed, 'thanks.' I try to move, but my head spins and my body doesn't respond. I touch my forehead, sweat is dripping down my face, the bed feels soaked.

Daniel and Gabriel were stood by the window.

'Morning,' I manage to croak, 'didn't see you there Daniel.'

Both men looked concerned for me, why? I really didn't have a clue.

Daniel comes to sit at the end of the bed, I cringe at the thought he may get wet.

Gabriel comes to within a foot of the bed and he looks as if he is towering above me, 'You're ill.' He says, his voice full of worry.

I feigned surprise, 'Really?' I let out a feeble giggle, 'Never!'

Gabriel stared at me, it was a look that could kill, 'I think you have a fever.'

Before I can retaliate; Daniel asks, 'Do you think you could stand up for a minute? We gotta change the bedding, it's not nice to be laying in it.' Daniel smirks.

My head felt clouded; I was almost certain I could manage that little task. As I start to move, Gabriel came over and stood no more than two feet from me. 'I can manage.' I croaked, 'Might take me a while.'

By now I had managed to sit at the edge of the bed. As I stand up, the room starts to spin wildly, I can feel my legs buckling beneath me. Before my body hits the floor, Gabriel caught me. His skin is ice-cold, which was a relief to me, as my own skin is burning like wild fire. I'd never noticed before; his eyes were no longer butterscotch, they were a deep burnt gold bordering on dark, contact lenses maybe?

'Daniel, hurry up,' He barks, 'she can't handle being here much longer,' his voice turns from angry to fret and worry, 'just hang on.' Gabriel looks at me with pain filled eyes.

Why? Was he scared for me? I thought he hated me?

Things seem to go hazy around the edges, two voices are heard whispering away.

'Look at the state of her.' One of the voices growl.

'Well, it's what we look like when we're not well, most humans sleep it off.' The other voice snaps back.

'I'll stay with her, she needs to cool down and my body is cold, it may help.'

'Good idea, I'll open the window, to let some cool air through.' Daniel replies to Gabriel.

The other voice shakes with anger and concern, 'How did this happen?'

'Will you keep it down,' orders Daniel, 'She was out in the rain for ages and naked for God knows how long, it must have happened then. Now calm down.'

A pair of cool hands cupped my cheeks, ah such bliss. A second later someone's entire body contacted my own, sheer heaven.

Now I didn't know if I was dreaming or not, but I could hear voices whispering in urgent tones about something important.

'Michael what can we do?' A voice asks in desperation.

'As Daniel explained to you already, there isn't a lot we can do. Daniel, there is a thermometer in the bathroom, I need to take her temperature.'

Something weird gets gently pushed into my mouth.

'Lydia, we are taking your temperature.' A voice reassures me.

I feel as if I'm falling deeper and deeper into the fog, an alarmed voice brings me back, monetarily.

'So, what is her temperature?' The voice sounded so close that if I lifted my hand up into the air I could touch them.

'It's impossible,' Michael quizzes, 'the thermometer says forty-three degrees Celsius.'

'WHAT?' Shouts a third voice, it had to have been Daniel.

'Now what can we do?' Gabriel asks in a panic.

'Hope she pulls through, it isn't natural for someone to have that kind of temperature, usually at this point they'd be dead, she seems to be defying the odds.'

The voices become echoes, before fading completely. I am falling through the fog.

Reality or not, I am alone, I felt cold, abandoned and most of all - scared.

Not knowing where I was made me shake with fear. This place felt foreign and devoid of comfort.

Out of the fog, a voice calls my name. I want to run, I want to hide, yet I feel rooted to the spot.

The ground beneath me gives way and once again I find myself falling, fearing reaching the bottom.

Someone's strong arms catch me as I fall.

'What in the hell is this place? Where am I?' My voice echoes in my mind, 'Am I dead?' I dare not turn around to face my saviour, not yet.

My rescuer answers, his voice is all too familiar, 'This fog is all in your mind, it's how clouded and confused you are. As to where you are, this realm is neither for the dead nor the living, merely a place between, where we are able to communicate,' He asks, 'Look at me Lydia, please.'

His tone seems urgent. Taking a deep breath, I turn my head, only to be staring into the eyes of my father, my limbs go numb, tears stream down my face like a cascade. My arms wrap around his shoulders, 'Oh dad,' I cry, 'can it really be you?'

There he was, standing there, cradling me. His green eyes stare back at me, he hadn't aged a day, his muscular arms wrap around me, still as steady as a rock. I never realised just how much I missed him, until now. I never wanted to let go of him.

He gently places me on the ground, my arms refuse to let go.

'This is serious my dear, we don't have much time.' His tone is firm.

Wiping tears from my face, I look him in the eye, 'What are you on about?'

'There are things, that in time you will find out, neither me or your mother are proud of it, but we did what needed to be done,' He kisses my forehead, 'a secret we harbour, what I tell you next is vital.' His eyes bore into mine.

'Tell me.' I beg of him.

'Both me and your mother were born a long time ago, we were left to die somewhere on a hillside, thing is we didn't die. At another point-' he looks around, 'we were told that we were part of a select few, half immortals, it was carried in the genes, but like I say only a few of us had that gene-' he kisses my cheek, 'when you came along, we were delighted. We also knew you would be different from all of us' he takes a breath, 'our genes somehow combined and you my sweetheart are immortal, pure immortal,' there's urgency in his voice, 'I must go, whatever you find out in times to come, just remember we love you, always have and always will.'

The tears flow freely from my eyes, I don't have time to ask him questions, he is already starting to fade away, 'Goodbye.' I manage to whisper to his ever-fading outline.

'Goodbye.' He replies, it is barely audible.

Feint rumbles can be heard, my body shakes and once again I am falling. I didn't care anymore; my body was still. Landing hard on a surface I feel the sensation of being dragged backwards, the fog vanished; and I was left alone in the darkness.

Between me and the darkness, there was nothing, I began to sob.

Chapter 9 - **Heartbreak**

My eyes shot open; confused about where I am, I nearly cry out for help, until I realise I'm in my bedroom, soft light came in through the window. Taking a deep breath, I start to relax. Turning my head, I am staring into the eyes of Gabriel; He looks worn out.

'Hi.' I croak. Oh dear, I feel heat spreading through my cheeks.

Gabriel smiles, 'Hey sunshine.'

Damn, that's gonna make my cheeks blush even more, 'How long was I out?'

'Just short of two days.' He smiles brightly.

Oh god, I'm gonna melt if he smiles again.

Gabriel's voice sounds raw and emotional, 'You got us all worried for a while, thankfully Michael kept us calm.'

I stretch, 'It was scary being alone in the dark, I should be used to It, but that place felt desolate.'

'I'm glad you came around.' Gabriel's sudden smile radiated a warm feeling throughout my body and although I ached from head to foot, the fever had dissipated.

Michaels voice echoed from downstairs, 'Is she awake?'

'Yes,' Daniels voice booms, 'come and see.'

In an instant Michael arrives, 'How are you feeling dear one?'

'Achy, could murder a glass of ice water though.' My voice sounds rough.

Gabriel rushes off downstairs and a moment later he returns with a large glass of Ice water.

The cool liquid is soothing to my parched throat and refreshes my senses.

Looking into Gabriel's eyes, somehow, they'd changed colour, strange, could be tinted contact lenses I suppose? But why did he look to have slight bruising under his eyes?

Gabriel announces, 'Lydia, shortly I have to go out, I shall be back by the time a new dawn arrives,' He ruffles my hair which sends shivers down my spine, 'you should rest, the others are staying, so you will be in good company.'

'Why do you have to go?' I reply weakly.

Gabriel grabs my hand, 'During the time you've been ill, I never left your side, I need to-' He hesitates, 'rest and relax alone.'

It feels like the end of the conversation, so I nod my head and smile feebly, 'Can someone help me out of bed, I need to move'

Michael grabs a hold of me gently and helps me downstairs.

Less than half an hour later, I watch Gabriel walk out the front door, 'Bye' I wave.

He smiles at me, 'Goodbye for now sweet Lydia.'

Watching the news nonchalantly, not really thinking of anything in particular, until my dream comes back to haunt me. In my heart I knew it had been more than a mere dream.

Fidgeting uncomfortably on the sofa, I accidently grab the attention of Michael; Who sweetly sits next to me and puts his arm over my shoulder. Internally I shudder, his body temperature is ice cold, was everyone else's temperature the same?

'Anything wrong dear Lydia?' Michael's voice echoes softly in my ear.

'You have no idea.' My mind answers him, my mouth doesn't move. After a slight hesitation (and a debate) I answer in a tone I've never used, so soft yet cold and dark, 'This is where, so many times I die yet again, not physically, just mentally, maybe it's meant to be, maybe I'm not meant to get better with time.' His skin still feels ice cold and in my gut; I have a sinking feeling, like I'm about to discover something, something I shouldn't know anything about.

'Is that all?' He replies, almost as if he already knows the answer.

I scratch my head in both frustration and realisation, 'While the world sleeps, I search for a part of me that long since died.' I suck, in a deep breath, 'I'm nothing more than an empty shell, the spirit that resided here is dead, nothing remains but shattered dreams, dark motivations and an endless nightmare, something I cannot escape.' Quickly I dive into the kitchen, open the back door and light up a cigarette. I felt as if I was falling; forever falling through an endless hole.

In my mind I kept repeating these words - 'Empty shell, eternal night,' and 'broken.'

I didn't see Michael and Daniel standing at either side of me, they make me jump out of my skin.

'Whether you realise it or not Lydia, if your parents Shannon and Joseph were here, they would be heartbroken with the words you speak.'

Daniel stands there; dumbfounded and trying to find the right words but realises he has no words to speak, instead he returns to the living room.

This left me and Michael. He awaits an answer and I am lost for words. How did he know my parents? Had I met them before? If so, where? I try quickly to recall if I've ever seen their faces. It is of no use, 'What are you?' I stare blankly at the floor, 'And how did you know my parents?'

'What I am is irrelevant and how I knew your parents,' he stares directly at me, 'they showed me that what I am didn't mean I was a monster, that I could rise above it and I'd known them for what felt like centuries.'

The words; centuries and monster almost freeze me to the spot. What did he mean by monster? And centuries? What wasn't he telling me?

Looking into his eyes, I see nothing, but truth reflected in my own, 'Okay.' I could only think of that one word. My instincts were telling me yet more was to come, and I had to wait patiently.

Just before 7:00am Gabriel walks in through the front door. He no longer looked tired, maybe relaxation does the trick? Where is the bruising that had been evident under his eyes?

Gabriel looks directly at me, 'I see you have not slept.' Gabriel sits next to me and puts his arm around me.

Wow, this is strange, 'Hi to you too.' I chuckle.

Blanking out all the questions racing inside my mind, snuggle against Gabriel, geez his temperature is also icy cold. Forget it, I'm too tired to ask. Though I had stored the information safely for when the time is right.

Gabriel rests his head upon my head so gently, I hardly notice, 'Sleep my sweet, you will feel better for it.'

Quickly I grab a pillow and blanket, snuggle up to him once again and drift sweetly into unconsciousness.

Chapter 10 - Time for the truth

By 9:00am the following day I was wandering around the supermarket; supplies of food were running low and so was the beer. For six months I felt that little more dependent upon alcohol to drown out my fears and help me sleep. Since my guests had arrived, I'd hardly needed alcohol, it was starting to lose its grip. This time I grabbed a bottle of coconut rum and then went to find the coke.

Gabriel and Daniel were heading to the cinema, Michael headed for the main library on the outskirts of town. This left me, thinking mainly; About where life was headed and what I would do with my time. I can't spend the rest of my life cursing the world, but it seemed the only natural thing that came to me, I just need to give myself a bit more time, to breathe and move forward.

At the checkout I kept wondering; how did they know my parents? As well as piecing together my own thoughts, all of it seemed like a huge jigsaw, pieces scattered all over the floor, waiting to be put back into place.

What did they mean when they mentioned my parents wouldn't be happy to hear me speaking the way I did?

'Excuse me, miss.'

The checkout operator brought me back to the real world, 'Sorry, was miles away.' I smile a crooked wistful smile.

In the car park, whilst putting my shopping in the boot of the car, thoughts were raging. Maybe a coffee at the café across the road would make me forget long enough in order for me to return home in one piece?

It was the information they had given me, things that seemed to sound alarm bells in my head.

'Think logically woman.' I told myself, whilst staring at the empty cup.

The fact they'd mentioned my parents, how did they know my parents? How long had they been friends? And why hadn't I seen them before? What part did my parents play in all this? By mistake I broke the cup, immediately I cleaned up the mess called the manager, paid for the broken cup and coffee, followed by going back to my car.

Unpacking the shopping, it dawned on me that the boxes in the loft might harbor clues, if not answers to what I was searching for. It would have to wait a while longer; my hunger needed satisfying.

'Here goes.' I whisper to myself whist opening the loft hatch. Greeting me are the familiar scents of old leather and vanilla. A thousand different memories came flooding back at once, so much so, I almost fall off the ladders. Regaining balance, I clamber into the loft and look at the mass of boxes, 'Now to discover the mystery hiding somewhere in here.'

Grabbing the box nearest me, I'm ready to tear it open, it is then I realise, that I have to take my time with this. Carefully opening the box, it's the same box I opened a few days ago and had a quick nosey through. Emotions rush over me like a raging waterfall; forever replenishing the unbreakable cycle that is life.

Almost straight away my eyes graze upon an old photo, Mesmerised I stare at the photo; within the photo are the three people that turned up only a few days ago.

I knew my parents were half-immortals, I also knew I was immortal, but where did these people fit in? What were they? And why did I feel as if I'd known them in another life? Everyone looked happy, on the back was a date - August 19th, 1891.

For some reason I shuddered, looking at the photograph one more time, red eyes flash before me, followed by golden eyes.

Standing up, I understand what two of my guests are. My instincts told me I'd known all along, the cold skin, eye colour change and their marble like skin. 'Vampires,' I whisper to the photo, 'that's why Michael said he thought he was a monster and my parents showed him how to utilise the gift he'd been given-' Downstairs the front door closes.

Tears cascade down my cheeks, 'How stupid was I? How didn't I see this earlier?' My heart begins to race, not out of fear, rather out of realisation.

'Hello, anyone here.' Calls Daniel from the bottom step.

There I was; sat frozen to the floor, almost trance like, the loft room was swirling, and my mind is full of confusion, 'Why?' I wonder quietly.

Just as darkness starts to creep into the loft did I realise I'd been up here for a number of hours. A pair of icy cold hands lightly touch my shoulder blades, which sends me into shock, turning around I'm ready to fight, it was Michael.

'Ah sweet Lydia, how long have you been up here? You look like you have seen a ghost my dear.'

My eyes seem to give me away, I had to be an adult about this, no tip toeing, go straight in for the kill, 'I've worked out what you and Gabriel are,' I take such a deep breath I feel like passing out, 'You are vampires, both of you, but not like those in my dreams, you are a different kind of vampire.' There I'd said it.

His eyes give me a sense of reproach and sadness, he sighs, 'Yes,' he nods, 'are you scared?'

Shrugging my shoulders, I answer, 'I don't think I'm scared, I am confused.'

By now Gabriel and Daniel were at the bottom of the ladders staring up.

All eyes are on me, I can feel them digging deeper into me, I had to escape the loft, jumping out of the loft I land on my feet and walk downstairs, not caring if they followed or not.

In the living room, no-one spoke for what feels like an eternity. We stood there like stone statues, though my heart was beating furiously, I could hear blood rushing through my ears and if I concentrated, I could hear the owls in the woods not far away.

Gabriel was first to break the everlasting silence, he stared directly at me, 'Do you hate us?'

Standing up I am within three inches of Gabriel, I want him to see the truth in my eyes, 'It's not a question of hate Gabe, feels as if there's a bond between us all,' I know my next move, 'I have to get away from here, to think clearly, I know what I must do, but a neutral place will be refreshing,' I repeat, 'I have to get away from here, too many memories to cloud my judgement.'

Fate rested with me, it was my choice, I had to make the call.

Now the atmosphere seemed more relaxed than previously.

Chapter 11 - The Emerald Isle, land of the lost and found.

Late afternoon the following day, Daniel and I are playing cards in the kitchen, whilst Gabriel and Michael spoke in hushed whispers about (what sounded like) where they would hunt next. Everything I'd learned so far had me in a state of confusion.

'Why is everything so complicated?' I mutter to myself as Daniel put his card down.

'Not everything in life is so complicated.' Whispered Daniel with a smile.

'Damn, a black jack, time to pick up five.' I mused.

The empty silence became unbearable, I wandered into the room to put a CD on. As I put it into the player, Gabriel stepped in front of me, 'I see you like Enya.' He grinned.

'I do, such soothing music and such an ethereal voice.' With that I went into the kitchen to continue playing cards.

It wasn't long before I'd gathered everyone into the room, they needed to hear what I was about to announce, 'I've made a choice,' taking a deep breath I smile weakly and carry on, 'I desperately need to think, but not here, gonna quit my job and take a flight outta here, you're all welcome to stay here whilst I'm gone,' quickly I turn my eyes to Gabriel, 'I'm not running away, staying here would only confuse things further.' There, I'd said it.

Michael hugs me and whispers in my ear, 'Truly I understand sweet Lydia, there is much to consider, more so for you, I doubt we could stay here in your absence.'

'I'd like it very much if you did, that way I wouldn't come back to an empty house and if my parents were here, they'd insist on you staying.' I unwrap my arms from around him and park myself on the floor.

Gabriel's eyes pierced mine, 'Do what you have to.' He muttered in a monotone voice.

Deep down I knew he'd react this way, I sit quietly on a chair.

Stepping outside I ring my boss at home, (he won't like that but I don't care) I explain that I'm quitting as of now due to personal reasons, he swears at me down the phone, I tell him exactly what I think of him, 'You're a trumped up stupid man, who thinks just because he has a little power, he can control the world, well guess what? Shove the job up your arse where even God himself wouldn't dare look.' With that I put the phone down, not caring about his reaction. Quietly I begin to chuckle, soon enough I'm laughing loud enough to wake the dead.

Instead of ringing the airport I book my flight on-line, 'One week will be enough.' After I'd checked out and paid I potter around the garden for a few minutes before heading back indoors to begin packing.

By the time I'd finished, Michael had arranged for me to stay with a friend of his, who owns a hotel just outside Dublin, 'Thanks.'

'You are welcome dear Lydia.' Michael softly replies.

At 9:00am I was on my way to the airport, Gabriel insisted upon driving me there, neither of us spoke to one another. It was a silence infused ride.

Getting out of the car I never glanced back, I was afraid to, then I heard the screeching of tyres, sighing I wander into the airport.

By 11:00am the flight took off, although my spirit started to relax, my heart felt as though it were missing something.

I arrived in Dublin around dinner, the smell of a City; a City full of life and energy which made me feel energised, it was a rather strange sensation.

Dropping my stuff off at the hotel I start to wander around this glorious City. My senses take in fresh scents, sights and sounds, not to mention plenty of bars offering true Irish drink and cuisine.

Tempted by traditional Irish music coming from one of the bars, I duck my head inside, I feel I've been transported to another time, the music sweeps over me and before I know it, my feet find rhythm I thought I never had.

10:00pm, the City had really come into its own, I opted for walking over the bridge that spanned the river Iffy, I was on my way to one more bar to enjoy one more pint of Guinness before heading back to the hotel for the night.

I found a bar, right on the corner, finding myself a seat I sup my Guinness, happily watching the world go by.

As midnight approaches I take one last lung full of air before heading to the hotel.

The guy on reception hands me the key to my room and bade me goodnight.

Inside the room I undressed, brushed my hair and crawled into bed, sleep came on swift wings.

8:00am, as Dublin was as lively as ever, I woke up from a dreamless sleep, feeling refreshed and ready for the day ahead. Getting dressed I take one last look at myself in the mirror, 'Not bad, time to go.' And head for the front desk.

The receptionist greets me with a smile, 'Good morning, are you checking out?'

'Yes please, is there a bus that runs to the train station?'

'Aye, there is, turn right when you go out of the door, take next right and there is a bus stop, the bus will take you to the train station.'

I rub my hands, 'Thank you, here are the keys, was lovely staying here, time to find breakfast, thanks bye.'

'Goodbye miss.' She hollers as I head out of the door.

I'd figured out I could get a train to Belfast, stay there all day, wait for night and then head further North-West towards the Giants causeway, I would have to research a place to stay somewhere near the causeway, to make it easier for me.

My phone rings just as I enter a café, 'Hello.'

'Hello dear Lydia, hope you enjoyed your stay?'

It was Michael, 'It was lovely, thank you, I'm just heading North to Belfast, after I've had breakfast.'

'Ah the troubled yet wonderful Belfast, haven't been there for over a hundred years.'

'Wow, how is everyone?' I enquire whilst stuffing my face.

'We are all good thank you for asking,' there's a slight pause, 'I will speak to you again sweet Lydia, enjoy the sights and if you ever feel lonely, you can always ring me.' He replies with sincerity.

I'm almost speechless, 'Thank you, okay have a fun week, bye for now.'

Now it is time to catch the train, which should arrive at the platform in ten minutes. The journey will take over two hours, the train takes the scenic route.

I could see why they called it the Emerald Isle. We passed little cottages and run-down barns, fields full of crops, vast wide-open spaces full of animals and little farm houses.

We passed the industrial area; run down and derelict, it looked like a ghost town.

Children were playing chase through empty buildings and I couldn't help but smile. It looked like the simple life, no cares, no worries, just you and a bunch of friends playing chase.

Finally arriving in Belfast, it was time for a big meal, then to wander around for a while before heading for another bite to eat, it was then I'd head North-West, firstly to ring the Bayview hotel to make a booking.

Booking complete, the Bayview in Portballintrae would be my home for a few days.

Food eaten and now I'm wandering around the local markets, people selling their wares and plying their trade.

Night falls upon Belfast and I am still awe struck by its beauty and history. Another hour and I would head North-East, find shelter for a few hours, as I would need my rest.

Time for a pint of beer and food.

By 4:00am I had reached Portballintrae, finding a piece of abandoned land, I change, put clothes on and find somewhere to rest until later in the day, 'I hope no-one sees me, they may think I'm homeless.' I chuckle to myself before curling up in a near-by farmers barn, using my bag as a pillow I close my eyes waiting for sunrise.

Chapter 12 - I am on fire, no seriously I'm on fire.

By the time I'd checked into the Bayview Hotel, dropped my stuff off, had a shower, changed, it was almost 3:00pm. My stomach growled so loud, people looked around thinking there was a dog hiding under their tables.

I sat there alone, basking in the late afternoon sun coming in through a large window, waiting for my meal to arrive.

Scents wafted from the kitchen; root vegetables, which I assumed was part of a stew, Guinness and steak pie and a delightful lemon mousse all mingled together in harmony.

As the waiter made eye contact, my eyes move up at such speed, I thought they were going to pop out of my sockets; not because he was attractive, but because he sent a chill down my spine and I couldn't fathom why.

'Your meal ma'am' He said as he placed the plate in front of me.

Quickly I closed my mouth and replied, 'Thanks.'

'My name is Morgan; my father owns this place.' He replies quietly.

I extend my hand, 'Lydia and I definitely don't own this place.' I start laughing at my own joke.

Morgan also begins to laugh, 'I'll be around if you need anything.' With that he wanders back, weaving his way around the tables, still chuckling to himself.

Stretching before me was the most magnificent coastline I'd laid eyes upon. Colours streaked the sky, waves lapped at my feet, I'd wandered to the Giants causeway to watch the sunset. A couple were just ahead of me, holding hands and whispering sweet nothings in each other's ears. Although I smiled, I also wished they would go away and leave me in this piece of heaven to enjoy, alone.

It is now dark and I am alone at long last, good, just the way I like it. If you closed your eyes, you could almost hear the voices of long ago. Right here right now, I could feel my parents nearby, if I held out my hand, I can almost touch them.

My heart beat a steady rhythm, the tide began to close in, I didn't want to move, but knew I had to, 'Just a few seconds longer.' I tell myself.

Walking back to the hotel, I think about the waiter. He looked around twenty-three, with dark green eyes, he was tall and his hair was light brown and messy.

Sitting in the quiet bar, I spy the waiter, (Morgan I think his name is) comes and sits down on the empty bar stool next to me. He looks more casual and relaxed.

'Can I buy you a drink?' He puts his hands up, 'Swear it, I'm not making a pass honestly.' Morgan smiles timidly.

He still gives me chills down my spine, I have no idea why? 'Okay, why not.' Gesturing to the seat next to me.

'What will it be?' Asks the barman.

'Pint of Guinness please.' I cheekily grin.

'I'll have the same.' Morgan replies.

A little while later, myself and Morgan have done nothing but talk, he asked about my family and what I'm doing here. I didn't have the guts to tell him I was alone in this world, that both my parents were dead and that I had come to clear my mind. Instead I tell him I'm in Ireland to trace family roots and that my family were scattered far and wide.

I then asked him about his family, what his ambitions were and what he wanted out of life, before we knew it, time had flown, the clock struck 1:00am. Morgan noticed I'm flagging, after a hot chocolate laced with Irish cream, he escorted me to my room and bid me goodnight.

'Goodnight.' I yawn.

Closing the door, I lay on the bed and soon fall asleep.

Sunrise the following morning, I'd perched myself on the window sill, mesmerised by the sun making its way slowly into the sky.

I eat my breakfast before heading to the causeway. As I went out of the front door, Morgan is there smoking a cigarette and he hands me a small package, 'For you.'

Peaking inside it is a picnic lunch, 'Thank you, that's sweet of you.' Oh no, my cheeks are starting to flush, this isn't fair.

'You're welcome, enjoy your trip.' He pats me on the shoulder.

'I will.' I step into the sun and start my walk.

The next four days are consumed by - my treks to the causeway, endless hours of wandering, of thinking and of my parents. Each afternoon was consumed by, more thinking of my parents, what I could do better, and would time go any faster? With each journey I felt a little more at ease but no closer to making a decision that was desperately needed.

Each evening would be taken up by; eating and talking with Morgan into the small hours of the morning.

It was on night four, my mobile rang, Morgan got up a little too quickly, saying he had something to do, I watched him storm off and I wasn't sure why he was in such a mood.

'Hello.'

'Hello sweetheart.'

Oh damn, it is Gabriel, why is he ringing? We parted on bad terms, 'How are you?' I enquire nonchalantly.

'I am okay thankyou and how are you doing?'

My heart wanted to blurt out that I was lonely, angry, confused and lost. My mind told me to stay calm and lie, there was no point making them worry, 'Not too bad thanks, not long to go and I'll be heading home.'

Gabriel could tell Lydia was missing home, 'Aw, home misses you too, as do we.'

Damn, that was a shock, 'You really are sweet.' My body was starting to relax, especially after hearing his voice, 'I'm no closer to a decision, I have no clue what to do.'

'Trust me, give it a little more time, it will happen.'

Sighing I know he is right, 'Thanks for the vote of confidence,' I look at the clock, 'didn't realise it was so late, gonna go now, will phone you when I land back in England.'

'Sleep well my lovely sweet Lydia, it was heavenly hearing your voice.'

Before I can reply the line goes dead, what the hell was that?

As the clock strikes 3:00am, I woke with a start. I had to get out, jumping out of the window I run as If I am running for my life.

By the time I stop running, realisation kicks in – I was near the causeway. Feeling my forehead, I knew I was burning up, there wasn't much I could do.

My hands try and cool my flesh down, but to no avail. The sensation of heat starts to increase, tears stream down my face, I wanted to scream, my throat seemed dry.

Once again, I look at my hands, they seem to be on fire, looking down; flames spontaneously ignite slowly, spreading over my body. I couldn't touch my skin, I was too afraid of the possible consequences.

Consumed by fire, I looked like a beacon in the night. There was nothing I could do: except stand there and allow the flames to eat at my flesh.

Chapter 13 - Oh please, not again! What is this? Test if Lydia is fireproof?

I awoke, finding that my back was aching terribly. Quickly scanning around I notice I'm on a high out-crop overlooking the Giants causeway, 'Shit.' I growl, luckily, I was secluded enough that no-one could see me.

'Were the early hours a dream?' I questioned whilst looking myself over, I felt fine, my clothes looked as they had done several hours ago. The heat had gone; leaving me feeling drained, looking at my watch I am amazed it was fast approaching 10:00am, 'Time to head back, I'm starving.' I slowly get to my feet and wander back to the hotel.

That night I dreamed of being on fire, of feeling the heat rise, flames licking at my body, taking my last breath as I burst into flames and then; somehow looking at the pile of ashes on the floor, the ashes that were once me. I wake up sweating, my breathing ragged I could hardly catch my breath. Looking at the clock, it was 3:00am, walking to the bathroom I take a huge gulp of water, great my mobile is ringing, shifting my clothes out of the way.

I answer it, 'Hi.' I'm still short of breath.

'What's wrong?' The voice on the other end of the phone was full of concern.

I'm close to tears, 'A fucking scary nightmare,' I mumble, 'I can't take it much longer.' It was then I realised I was talking with Gabriel I was confessing to, oh hell! How the hell did he know?

'I will take the next flight out, I don't want you on your own.' It sounded more like an order than a request.

I couldn't have him here, no matter how desperately I wanted him to fly over, plus it would might confuse matters, not to mention distract me, wiping the tears away I answer, 'Please don't, I don't have long until I fly home,' I take a deep breath, 'it was only a silly nightmare.' My body begins to shake at the mere thought of the previous night, I really was on fire and yet I survived.

'You don't sound alright and it doesn't sound like it was just a silly nightmare.'

There was no way I could confess to him that the previous night, I was ablaze, holding back the rising bile in my throat, 'Two more days, I'm sure I can handle that,' I add, 'dreaming of being on fire can confuse anyone.' Shit, did I really just say that?

'Fire?' Gabriel sounds confused, it is then he speaks, with deep regret and realisation, 'When you arrive home, we will be here to comfort you and to welcome you home.'

Damn, he's not saying everything he wants to say, something stirs within him and I cannot tell what, 'Thank you and thanks for calling, it is nice to hear from you.'

Gabriel starts chuckling down the phone, 'As always Lydia, you are most welcome, see you soon my angel.'

'Bye Gabriel.' I put the phone down only to clock on to the fact he called me angel.

Laying down on the bed I stare at the ceiling, waiting to drift off to sleep.

It is my final day near the Giants causeway, before heading back to Dublin for my flight home.

The previous night had been uneventful, in fact I'd spent most of the night talking with Morgan in his living room, just as the sun came up, he said something that I would never have expected, 'You are the saviour of this world, you are man's protector, you have walked many lives, seen many things and this time you are immortal.'

My drink of tea went cascading down my shirt, causing me to jerk in its brief heat, 'Pardon?' I was flapping my shirt.

'I will not repeat, I know you heard, but I will say this – your time will come.' Morgan stands up and offers me his shirt, 'Keep it,' he smiled, 'bit big though.'

Looking down at myself I chuckle, 'I suppose it is, but you can have it back some time, that I promise.'

Morgan's words plague me as I wander to the causeway for the final time. Just as I arrive, tourists are leaving, so I quickly decide to hide until the last of the tourists have gone.

Not more than an hour has passed, the tourists had gone. Stepping out of my hiding place I was in time to watch the sun set over the water, 'Such bliss.' I smiled to myself.

It must have been close to 10:00pm, I was the only human standing there, peering out into the darkness, the waves lapping playfully at my feet.

The heat began rapidly, spreading like wildfire through my body, 'Not again.' I scream.

Giant fiery wings spring from my shoulder blades, flames spread downwards towards my feet, the heat feels so strong I cannot overcome it. Sinking to my knees, the flames consume me like a fire consuming a forest.

In my pain, a voice echoes all around me, 'Do not fear the flames, embrace them my child.'

With all my might I cry out, 'I can't, it's too much.'

'Look within your soul my child, your choice is made, now you must embrace this mightiest of changes.'

In a moment of madness, I begin pounding at the ocean, trying desperately to hang on to what I know. The words my father spoke begin to sink in, 'I must see into my soul, I must embrace what is happening, in order to move forward.'

Closing my eyes; my life flashes before me, my heart begins to beat furiously, an image sticks, I have made my choice. The flames subside, I am left there; in the darkness, glimpsing at the moon, tears stream from my eyes. I drag myself to the hotel, I need some sleep, I want to forget what just happened, for now at least.

Stirring in my bed, I wake up feeling somewhat exhausted but at the same time; I knew my choice had been made. A great change had taken place. It was as though I had accepted a part of me I didn't even know, a feeling from deep within was telling me, soon enough I'd come to know this new part of me.

'Today I have to head home.' I muttered as my heart sank a little at having to leave this paradise.

Chapter 14 - I'm home.

Finally, Manchester airport is in sight. About time too, there had been some late boarders, so that meant the flight had been delayed.

After half an hour of waiting for my bag to pass me on the carousel, it was time to leave the airport and find Daniel.

'Wonder where he is?' I crane my neck to see above people's heads, still no sign of him, 'I suppose he's waiting outside.' Dragging my bag, I head for the doors to the outside world.

As I exit the airport, I see Gabriel's smiling face, he grins at me like he hasn't seen me in years. He is leaning against a hire car, 'So where is Daniel?' I mutter.

My feet stay planted as I try to work out what's going on. Walking forward I understand now, 'Time to greet the grumpy vampire.' I chortle quietly at my lame insult.

Placing my bag down I hug Gabriel, 'Thought Daniel was picking me up?' I let go and look up at him, then stare around me, girls are staring at him with intrigue, as they pass him they smile but he doesn't notice. Taking a step back, it seems he only has eyes for me.

Gabriel runs his thumbs up and down my cheeks before kissing my forehead, 'Change of plan, I'm so glad to see you.'

Okay, so that was weird, best go with the flow and not spoil the mood.

Grabbing my bag, Gabriel opens the passenger door for me, followed by taking the bag out of my hands and putting it in the back of the car.

'Thanks.' I smile as I put on my seatbelt.

'Did you have a nice time?' Gabriel asks without taking his eyes off me.

I didn't want to think about what had happened, 'Depends on what you class as a good time.' My body shudders.

With his eyes back on the road, he slips his hand in mine, as he does so, he flinched, and I feel the car accelerate.

'Why did you flinch?' I thought it was a harmless question.

'A strange sensation.' Gabriel half mutters.

I didn't like his answer, 'I can let go if you like?' I try to move my hand but Gabriel keeps it there intertwined with his.

'I'm not used to it but I like it.' He beams at me.

A sudden jolt of electricity runs through me, it wasn't bad, looking over at Gabriel, the same jolt had run through his body too.

Looking around, we're not heading straight home, 'Where are we going?'

'It's a surprise.' He winks and accelerates harder.

Thoughts of curiosity and excitement circle my mind.

My eyes adjust to the fading light, it looks like we have arrived wherever Gabriel wanted to take me. We pull up outside a café, 'Time to eat my lovely.' Gabriel offers me his hand.

'I could have waited until I got home.' My cheeks begin to flush.

'I know, but I wanted some time with you, without anyone else being around.'

Okay now my cheeks are glowing red. I bet you could use me as a light and see me in the dark.

He helps me out of the car, puts his hand on the small of my back and leads me into the café.

An hour later, after a quick bite to eat and a chat, we are heading home. Gabriel's sweet humming sends me into a lull, soon enough I'm drifting off to sleep.

Next thing I know, Gabriel is whispering in my ear, 'You're home.'

Gravel crunches under me, but I am too tired, all I want is my bed.

Daniel and Michael are in the living room waiting to greet me, Gabriel takes me in his arms, 'Not long and you can sleep.'

His sweet breath lingers on my taste buds, 'Cheers.' I reply as we walk into the living room, 'Hi you two,' I greet my two guests, 'I'm so tired,' I wrap my arms around them both, 'sorry to be rude, I need my sleep.'

'It is okay Lydia, we will speak in the morning.' Michael replies.

'Night.' Daniel waves.

Gabriel tucks me up in bed, 'Sleep well my sweetness, see you in the morning.' He kisses my forehead.

The smell of fresh coffee brings me to the land of the living.

'Home sweet home.' I mutter blissfully.

'How was your break?' Michael asks.

May as well get on with it, Gabriel hands me a coffee, 'Thanks.'

Squiggling in bed until I feel comfy, then I begin, 'The scenery was spectacular, it took my breath away,' sighing I continue, 'I met a guy, he is the son of the owner of the hotel I stayed in, something about him gave me the creeps but he kept me company without distraction,' I knew I had to tell them one of the scariest things that'd ever happened to me, 'throughout my time there, I was no closer to a decision, waking up at 3:00am with fever and wanting to run,' my heart beat faster, 'so I ran, it was then I caught fire for no reason, I couldn't scream, instead I stood there, praying that it would be over with, I woke up on some rocks early the next morning,' my entire body starts to tremble, even recalling the event sent me wild with fear, 'that night I dreamed about been on fire, my soul escaped and watched my body burn then turn to ashes,' looking around the room, Daniels eyes were filling with tears, Gabriel was on his knees bowed over and Michael looked as if he wanted to give me a hug to make me forget this experience, 'don't feel sorry for me, I guess it was something that needed to happen,' back to the matter at hand, 'I felt torn and twisted, my final night, it happened again, I ran, just as I did two nights previously, in my torment my father's voice called to me, I had to embrace the change, as I stood there consumed by flames, fiery wings sprung from my shoulder blades, what my father had said sank in, the flames died away.' That was my story, my decision had been made and, in my heart, I knew it was the right choice.

My three guests look at me, I smile in return, they knew what choice I'd made, there was no need to ask, it exuded from my soul.

Rubbing my hands, I ask, 'What shall we do today?'

Chapter 15 - **Time to go out and about**

'You know full well that isn't fair.' I cry out.

The vampires were leaving later tonight to hunt, Daniel was going with them as he said he wanted to explore a little.

Gabriel was adamant that I wasn't going, that I couldn't see monsters hunt.

'Look,' I stare at Gabriel sternly, 'I know I don't need to hunt but I want the freedom, you can leave me in the nearest pub, when I've had enough I'll come find you.'

Gabriel's expression is unreadable, his fists are rolled so tight I can see his even whiter knuckles standing out against his flawless skin. He stands with his back against the wall and his arms folded, 'Okay, fine but do not let trouble find you, it seems to have a way of following you.'

'HA!' I snorted, 'How am I gonna get into trouble?' Before he has time to answer, I jump in with one final comment, 'It's not like we're dating or owt, is it?'

His features became more rigid than they had been a moment ago, oops, wrong move, well it was true.

'As I have already stated, trouble follows you and you can be careless.' His tone was both angry and concerned.

Standing up I am inches from his face, 'That's what life's all about; risks, taking chances and anyway, my life I'll do as I please.' With that I sit back on the sofa, smiling like a Cheshire cat. Looking across at Michael I whisper, 'Are all vampires this moody?' A chuckle escapes my lips.

'Not at all my dear, it would seem Gabriel is the only one.' His eyes light up and a smile spreads across his face.

Even Gabriel joins in with a hint of his beautiful smile.

An hour or so later, we are on the road.

'Where we headed?' I enquire.

'The Dales,' Daniel replies, 'the way Gabriel drives, it's a wonder there's any car left.' He lets out a snicker, putting his hand over his mouth still chuckling.

We pull up outside a country pub, damn, I think this is where I'm getting out. The engine is silent.

'What are you all doing?' I feel slightly more than confused.

Gabriel stands behind me, rests his chin on my shoulder and points to what looked like dense woodland and a massive set of hills, 'We're heading in that direction, easier for the car if it stays here, we should be back before dawn, but please come and find us before going anywhere.' Gabriel's voice sounds magical.

'Okay, hope you all have fun.' I spin round and, in an instant, the three figures have vanished.

The pub has a lovely atmosphere, it is quaint, old fashioned, they even have a wood burning fire, ah such bliss, 'Can I have a coke please?' I ask the cute barman.

I pay for my drink and find somewhere to sit, near the raging fire.

To the right of me are a few old men, having what looked like a card game, they were chattering and throwing the odd insult at one another.

My current surroundings suited me, the pub wasn't packed, yet it wasn't dead, each old oak beam screamed history at me. The interior was modest, old fashioned which seemed in keeping with the age of the building.

My eyes begin to droop as I settle into the comfy leather chair near the fire, something I see for just a second brings me round again, looking at my watch it is close to 9.30pm, 'Still enough time for another ice-cold drink to keep me awake.' I head to the bar and order not one drink but two, an ice-cold coke and a steaming hot mug of coffee, 'thanks.' This time I sit away from the open fire, but I can hear the logs crackling away.

After a while my mobile rings, 'Hello.'

'Hi, we could be a while longer, when you're ready we are seven miles East of you, leave the car.' Daniel sounds breathless.

'Okay, see you shortly.' I hope.

Quickly finishing my coffee, I walk out of the pub and stare into the darkness, 'Which way is East?' I ask myself, before looking upwards to see if that would be of any help. I'm no good with directions in places I don't know, it is an oddity, I know.

Standing under the pubs only street light, I light up a cigarette.

Suddenly my heart kicks up a gear, I feel a sense of urgency, throwing my cigarette onto the floor, I look behind me, a pair of shadowy wings spring from my shadows shoulder area, I feel as if there are protective hands wrapped around me, I feel a sense of panic. I wander into the darkness, hoping I can erase these feelings from my mind.

Ten minutes later, I know I'm lost, in the distance are specks of light, most likely street lights in a town or village, luckily, I always carry a torch with me, grabbing it, I switch it on, there is a second shadow, much taller than me, wherever I stepped, the tall shadow stepped with me, taking a deep breath, I run as fast as I can towards the lights in the distance. Still I cannot shake the feeling of being followed.

Feeling dizzy and out of breath, I lean against a street light shaking like a leaf. Sinking to my knees, I see the tall shadow towering over my own. Stretching its hands towards my shoulders, I feel the slightest of tingles, although I'm scared to death, I also begin to feel calmer. Looking around there is no-one behind me, 'Maybe I'm losing it.' The question swims in my mind.

Wings spring from the tall shadow, the wings must span at least three metres, mesmerised I stare open mouthed at the shadow and for a moment I feel weightless, as if I'm floating on air. In an instant the shadow fades, leaving me dazed and light-headed.

I'd now lost track of time, I had switched my mobile off, in case I got robbed, squinting at my watch it's 1:45am, 'Shit.' I grumble just as a large twig trips me up, sending me flying into the darkness, 'this is gonna hurt.' I think quickly, but before I can act, a pair of cold marble like arms catch me, inches from the ground.

'Damn,' I think, Gabriel places me back on my feet, 'thanks.'

His voice is both dark and broody, 'I told you to come find us, not wander into the darkness.'

He puts his hands on my shoulders, sending chills down my spine.

'I didn't mean to, something happened-' I didn't get any further.

'Tell me, now.' His voice is low and gruff.

How do you tell people you saw shadows? I'll give it my best shot, 'Okay,' I realise it will be easier to explain on the way home, 'I'll tell you in the car, come on let's go.'

Gabriel sits with me in the back of the car, 'Now tell me.' He says.

Looking at him I begin, 'It began in the pub, just for a second I thought I saw something, when it came time to find you, I couldn't remember which way East was,' breathe, 'anyway a shadow followed me, it wasn't just any shadow, this thing had wings.'

Gabriel and Daniel burst out laughing, this angers me to bursting point, whilst gritting my teeth, 'Michael, please pull over.'

The car comes to a halt, I jump out of the car, I'm almost foaming at the mouth, 'God damned morons,' I yell, 'I swear to you a shadow followed me, it had wings and to top things off, I felt I was floating on air.'

Gabriel is still laughing, Daniel has stopped chuckling and stands rooted to the spot.

'Tell you what then, you guys take the car home, I'll walk, I'm not,' glaring at Gabriel, 'been sneered at by you, I know what I saw, and I know how I felt.' Crossing my arms, I stand there waiting for an answer.

Seriousness crosses Gabriel's face, when he looks into my eyes he sees that I am telling the truth.

'I'm sorry, please ride home with us.' Gabriel whispers.

'Fine, but next time I tell you something, take it seriously.'

In the car we get, the engine roars to life and we are on the road home.

Chapter 16 - **Getting to know me, getting to know you**.

The following morning, I'm downstairs eating breakfast and I'm mystified at the events of last night, I could no longer shake the feeling that no matter where I went, someone or something was keeping an eye on me.

'Morning sunshine.' Gabriel says happily.

'Morning.' I reply with a gob full of cereal.

A sudden wave of excitement rushes through me, 'So, tell me about yourself.'

He sits facing opposite me, 'Are you sure you want to know?'

'You tell me about how you came to be and later, I'll tell you about me, we can go for a walk or something.' My heart feels as if it is ready to break.

'Okay, deal.' He shakes my hand but doesn't seem to let go. 'I was born in seventeen fifty-five in North Dakota, two years before the start of the seven years' war,' he was making sure I was listening, 'I grew up in reasonable comfort, one event was to change me, because my mother was British, she was hung by a vengeful American man who accused her of witchcraft, which wasn't true, he liked her but, she wanted nothing to do with him that is why he despised her so much,' I could feel the anger flowing out of him, still he continued, 'she was hung on July 7th seventeen seventy-four in the main town, my thirst for revenge burst open like a volcano exploding, in August of seventeen seventy-five, I joined the army, to fight against our oppressors, whilst writhing in agony after being shot, Michael found me on the floor, he dragged me away and whispered in my ear, "I'm sorry" with that he bit me.'

I felt horrified, agonised and sorrow, 'I'm so sorry.' was all I could think of to say.

He smiled but it didn't radiate warmth, 'It was not your fault.'

'So, what was your real name?'

'Alexander Gabriel Peters, afterward I adopted my middle name and Michael's last name.'

Opening the back door, I ask, 'How did it all feel?'

'For a few decades I was resentful of my new life, I missed my mother, I watched my father die at the hands of British invaders. After 1817, I began to accept who I was and came around to Michaels way of thinking.' This time he smiled his captivating smile, sending my mind into a spin. With that he grabbed my hand and led me outside.

After a few miles we stopped walking, a picnic was already waiting, 'How did you manage all this?' I ask.

'It's nothing really, sit please.' He gestures for me to sit on the blanket.

Laying down on the blanket, I stare at a crystal blue sky, only Gabriel's cool hand brought me back to reality, 'Sorry, I was miles away.' My eyes still stare at the sky.

'How are you?' He asks.

Sighing and staring into his eyes, 'Restful and quite relaxed.'

His smile fades, 'Now it is your turn to tell me all about you.'

In an instant I am bolt upright, his smile faded, but I did promise, here goes, 'My name is Lydia Shayne Chambers, I was born June 13th around tea time, I grew up in the house I still live in,' breathing deeply I continue, 'went to college after high school, learned to play guitar at an early age, from college I went to Uni, from there it goes downhill,' my heart started to race, 'my first year at Uni passed without incident, I came home for the summer and enjoyed feeling young again, I managed to get a job working in an office, went back for my second year,' I can feel my body shaking, 'two weeks off for Christmas break, heaven, so I got my stuff together, jumped in the car and I was heading home,' I had to pull all my strength together, so I didn't fall apart, for a second I questioned if I should continue, it was then, whilst looking at Gabriel, he had told me his story, crossing my legs I breathe, 'halfway home a family friend called Ben phones me, he is in tears, I tell him to give me a few minutes as I'm near the services, obviously I'd pulled over to answer the call,' I'm really feeling edgy now, 'I grab a coffee and a bite to eat at the services and ring him back, he'd found my parents dead in the lab a few hours ago, the bodies were taken for a post mortem, but I had to go ID them,' tears fill my eyes and rage seethes beneath my skin, 'their funeral was held and I was left devastated, I finished Uni the following summer and went to work in an office.'

Gabriel held me in his arms, trying to calm me down, in amongst my fits I manage to mutter, 'Someone murdered them I know it.'

'Sweetheart, Shhhh, calm down, you're alright, I won't ever let anyone hurt you, never.'

After I'd calmed down; we continued the picnic, something Gabriel mentioned earlier springs to life, 'What did you mean by what you said earlier?' I didn't want to jump to conclusions.

Without warning Gabriel kisses me full on the lips, my legs give way as I feel I am being swept into paradise. A moment passes, and he sets me on the floor gently, looking deep into my eyes he whispers in my ear, 'My sweet Lydia, you do not see it, do you?'

Confusion sweeps across my face and into my voice, 'See what? Have I missed summat?'

He chuckles, 'Silly,' his voice turns serious, 'from the moment I saw you, I knew I had found my soul mate, my one and only.'

Holy hell, he is serious, my throat dries out, I try to find my voice, 'Wow, so I guess we're dating then?'

'For now,' he smiles wickedly, 'I will tell the-'

Michael and Daniel appear, Daniel hugs me and congratulates Gabriel, Michael hugs Gabriel and me.

We enjoy the rest of the picnic I am feeling so happy and lost for words, at last, everything is slotting into place, I can't ask for more.

Chapter 17 - **Heartburn and over the mountains**

Here I am wandering around the local town on a warm sunny day. Actually, I'm here to pick up food supplies, since Daniel eats like a pig.

My confidence is at an all-time high, well it must be, people are staring and smiling at me as I waltz through the outdoor market.

I hear someone creeping up on me, quickly turning around, I'm face to face with a sweet smiling man, 'Sorry.' I manage to say quietly.

'You look radiant.' The stranger replies.

I begin to blush, just when I'm ready to reply he's gone. I let my eyes slide for a second and in that second, I can't see him anywhere, 'What is going on?' I muse and then carry on shopping.

In the car, with the radio full blast, windows down, the wind whisking through my hair. Looking in the rear-view mirror; someone is sat on the back seat, pulling over, and cutting the engine, still the guy is sitting in the back, 'Who the hell are you?' I growl.

'You might wish to rephrase that question.' The guy smiles back.

I'm not sure if I should smack him, that is tempting right now, 'What are you doing in my car?' My mood is changing rapidly.

His voice reminds me of a harp, 'Observing.'

Okay, now I'm pissed off, keeping my tone even, 'By the time I get on the road again, you best not be there,' something clicks, 'you, it's you, the guy from the outdoor market.' My eyes stay glued to him.

'Maybe, maybe not.' He shrugs.

He kisses my forehead and the lights go out.

For some reason I feel sea sick, my body is being jerked around. Fluttering my eyes until they stay open, outside it is dark and by the feel of it; going over speed humps, what the hell is happening?

Staring forward, Daniel is driving my car, Michael is in the passenger seat, turning my head I stare into a pair of bronze eyes, Gabriel of course, he has an arm wrapped around me.

'What's going on?' I cry groggily.

'Honey, we found you passed out in the passenger seat, we were all worried, we came looking for you.'

Stretching my neck and arms, I remember what happened earlier, 'There was a guy in the car, I asked what he was doing, he didn't answer the question, I remember being annoyed coz no-one was there when I got in the car,' yawning loudly, 'he kissed my forehead and the world went black.' That part confuses me, mainly because the stranger appeared in my car.

Gabriel's growl rouses me from momentary confusion.

'A stranger was in your car?' Gabriel is annoyed, frantically he is sniffing the air.

'He wasn't there, but I did see him in the outdoor market, he complimented me.'

'If I ever get a hold of him, hell will not stop me ripping him to shreds.' Gabriel's response is final.

Back home we all play cards into the early hours.

I can't believe they're all leaving me alone for a few days. All three want to explore Scotland, damn it, I wanna go too.

'The break from us will do you good.' Gabriel is trying to reassure me.

I suppose he's right, faking a smile, 'I'm sure I can occupy myself.'

'Settled.' Wails Daniel, punching his fist into the air.

'That is that then, we leave at dusk.' Michael smiles warmly.

My heart sinks as the thought of loneliness begins to encroach.

Just after dusk, I'm on my own and bored brainless, 'Maybe a DVD will help pass the time?' I muse before picking a DVD and sticking it in the machine.

A while later and I'm pondering what to do with my given time alone, lighting a few scented candles, I turn the TV off, and sit on the floor cross legged trying to relax.

From no-where; a belch creeps up on me and escapes with such force I think I've been sick, 'Must have been the curry repeating on me.' Looking at the now blank TV screen I see a bunch of people huddled together next to a raging fire, one of them looks directly at me, smiles, bows his head and turns back to the others in the group. The image fades away, 'What the hell was that?' I openly ask thin air.

Blowing out the candles I think no, this time alone isn't working, I need to get out onto the moors, maybe I won't feel so alone then?

Out on the moors; I never feel alone, it is as if someone is standing right beside me, although I can't see them, touch them, or hear them, I feel whoever it is and that's enough for me.

Surrounded by darkness, I am more in possession of my mind, only the wind whistling around me can be heard, I am away from civilisation and on the edge of the stars.

A roar echoes in the distance, 'What was that?' I whisper to myself.

Again, the roar echoes, this time much closer, the moon peeps out from behind the clouds giving the moors an ethereal edge. Inhaling through my nose to calm myself down, as the air exits my mouth, a fireball exits too, I shout, 'This isn't funny.' to no avail, no-one is here except me.

Taking another deep breath in, a fireball escapes, one step forward and I feel a change coming, closing my eyes, I block out the world, I am encased in my world of fire; suddenly the image disappears, I'm looking directly into a large eye, 'Oh dear God.' I mumble, just as the moor vanishes from my feet.

Waking up surrounded by darkness, my heart is a steady rhythm and I feel more alive than ever. Standing up so I can stretch, I notice I'm higher off the ground than usual, trying to work it out, I need to scratch my head, only to find I haven't got fingers any more, looking down at myself, the physical self-had changed. Not that I knew what, 'Who or what the fuck am I?'

In a microsecond my mind was calculating creatures that were this tall. Looking down, my arms are slightly smaller than my legs, behind me are a set of wings, 'HOLY SHIT.'

I'd worked it out, there was only one creature tall enough and the only one that had wings as powerful as these - dragon.

'The gang has to see this,' I hum with delight, 'but, which way is Scotland?'

Smelling the air, their scents are strong in the air, 'Follow my nose I guess.' Chuckling, I take to the skies.

The views from up here are beyond stunning; the stars are shining brightly, the Earth looks magnificent from here, the odd cloud rolls over in the sky, yet we take it all for granted, for this opportunity I'm grateful, and take in each wonderful sight, sound and scent.

Before me stretches the outline of the Grampian's, time to head a little lower, so I can see the people I am after. My thoughts switch to Gabriel and how he would react to the way I look right now, a hilarious image flashes across my mind. By accident; I let out a half growl half chuckle.

Light was growing, night was fading, and I am losing hope of finding them before the sun starts to rise, heading for the ground, I land pretty gracefully, I turn around, at which point, three tiny people stop in their tracks.

'Yes, it's them.' I jump up and down with joy.

Daniel looks at me, firstly with anger then shock, 'Guys,' he points at me, 'that's Lydia.'

'Do I really look that bad?' I question myself.

'How do you know?' Gabriel asks, crouching down waiting to pounce.

'Don't,' Daniel warns, 'stand up, take a proper look.'

A few moments, all three are laughing and joking, I wonder if their laughter is delayed shock?

I didn't have time to think, the violent sneeze catches me unaware, sending me flying over the mountains, into the North Sea.

'YEOW,' that's freezing, only then did I realise; I was human once again, 'I NEED A HAND.' I shout with all my might just as my head sinks beneath the waves.

A hand grabs a hold of me, I was being dragged to dry land.

My mind swam with different thoughts, each competing for first place. It is in that moment I remember – I am immortal and cannot die.

Chapter 18 - I'm part of their family, with a strange connection

We arrive home just before 7:00am, wow had we really been away for over twenty-four hours? Gabriel places me gently on the sofa and wraps his arms around me.

'Do you ever sleep?' I blurt out, directing the question straight at Gabriel.

He looks at me with radiant bronze eyes, 'No,' he smiles, 'I occupy my time wisely and since meeting you I like to watch you sleep.'

Blood rushes to my cheeks, turning them bright red, Gabriel kisses my flushed cheeks, my smile gets wider and then begins to fade, 'How long before you guys head back home?' I know I don't wish to hear the answer, but I had to know how much precious time I have left with these wonderful people.

Michael answers the question without hesitation, 'Daniel has just over a week, his family are expecting him, as for us two, just under eight weeks.'

'Eight weeks?' I exclaim, I didn't mean to sound so upset.

'My dearest Lydia, excuse me, I need to see how things are back home.' With that Michael wanders outside to make his call home.

Eight weeks doesn't seem far, my soul is already feeling down and my mind in a daze.

As for my heart; too numb for words. For the first time in three years, I felt complete, without them I would simply fall to pieces, out of the corner of my eye I see Gabriel is smiling, 'What are you smiling at?'

'Michael is talking with Callum, he is happy we found you but it would seem he is a little reluctant to Michaels suggestion.' Gabriel smirks.

'What suggestion?' I'm now curious.

'Callum is seeing the sense in the suggestion and agrees it would be the best solution.' Gabriel's eyes sparkle.

Feeling more confused than before, I curl up and read a book.

I don't know how much time has passed me by, whilst looking over my book, Michael is sat on a chair staring and smiling at me.

'Are you hungry?' Michael stares directly at me.

'I'm good for now, thanks,' getting up from the sofa, 'but I do need some fresh air, excuse me.'

Sitting out back on a dining chair, I light up a cigarette and let the sun encase me in its everlasting warmth.

The cold touch of Michael's hand makes me turn around, only to see Daniel and Gabriel. Like I need more confusion right now.

'You look sad.' Daniel comments as he kneels in front of me.

So, like an idiot I blurt out, 'Soon you'll all be back home, I'll be here heartbroken and alone,' sighing, 'not the best feeling in the world.' I try to laugh, instead it comes out as a grunt.

'You are a part of this family, always will be.' Gabriel says as he puts his arm around my shoulder.

'Dear sweet Lydia, I was discussing with Callum, about you moving to America and living with us, as always though, it is your choice whether you wish to take that leap or not.' Michael smiles at me, his eyes shine with possibilities and warmth.

I feel as if the air has been knocked out of me, waves of emotions crash over me, I am delighted at the thought of moving somewhere new but at the same time, I was scared to leave the home I knew and loved. It was where I'd grown up and yet where my parents had spent their last day upon the Earth.

Looking at all three faces I feign a weak smile, 'There's much to consider, right now my mind is clouded.' I rub my temples, reeling from the shock.

'We want you to be happy, but most of all, we want you to be safe.' Michael goes to stand in the doorway.

'We'd have so much fun.' Daniel grins and steps to one side.

'My love, what we are trying to say is; we all love you, we want you with us so we can protect you, nurture you and give you a new lease of life, your parents would have wanted this, I am sure of it.'

I am in more shock than before, 'What job would I be doing?'

'I run and own a counselling therapy practice, there are many people who cannot be seen, because I do not have the staff, you would be an excellent asset'

'Well, I have degrees in psychology, forensic psychology and health studies.' The future is looking a little brighter.

'So, that will be your job, perfect for getting your visa and work permit for the states.'

'Much to think about.' I reply with an inward smile that could compete with the Sun.

As I walk out of the bathroom, Daniel is sleepily coming out of the spare room. 'Good nap?' I ask.

'Very good,' he stretches and yawns, 'amazing what a power nap can do.'

'We need to talk, but not here,' making my way downstairs, 'I'll take you out for some food, we can talk there and no you're not in trouble.' I wink and enter the front room.

'You read my mind, I'm starving.' Daniel grins.

'Have a coffee, then we can go, I'll even put the kettle on for ya.' I wander into the kitchen and put the kettle on.

Daniel sits at the kitchen table to wait for it to boil, with that I appear in the front room, and sit next to Gabriel, who looks a little down, 'What's up?'

'Why can't you discuss it here?' His voice sounds melancholy.

'Strange vampire,' I think to myself, in answer to Gabriel's question, 'because here it's a private place, in town it's open, public space, I feel at ease with him, plus I need his help in making up my mind.' I give him my most innocent smile.

My innocent look makes Gabriel laugh, 'Cheeky.' He says as he helps me to my feet, we begin dancing, this is so embarrassing but intimate. Time could pass by without a second thought. I wouldn't care, not one bit.

Half an hour later, both Daniel and I have made it into town. Around the corner from the main street is my favourite café. Opening the door, the scent of fresh roasting coffee greets us, we find a corner table.

After ordering, I turn to Daniel and ask, 'Should I move?' I felt lost and needed the truth.

With a mouthful of crisps he answers me, spraying me with crisps, 'Hell yeah, it'll be a new start for ya and we'd be able to better protect you.'

A shudder runs down my spine, that same connection that hit me when I first saw him, 'This sounds crazy but, do you think you and I have a connection?' I cringe in preparation for his answer.

He is about to answer, when our food arrives, 'Thanks.' I say to the waiter.

Daniel starts muttering, ending with a growl.

'What's up?' I'm puzzled as to his reaction.

'That waiter was eyeing you up,' he points with his fork, 'I wasn't happy, not at all.'

'Just eat the food, I didn't notice.' I dive right into my desert.

'I love you.' Daniel blurts out, stunning me into silence.

'Pardon?' I needed to make sure I'd heard him right.

'Me and you have a connection, dunno what or why but, yes I love you, from the moment I saw you, it's not that kinda love,' He winks, 'it's more like brother sister type love.'

A flash of a distant memory plays out in front of my eyes – two people sat in front of a fire, they are possibly husband and wife, she is getting ready for battle, he is now on his knees, pleading and begging her not to go, she hugs him tightly and whispers something in his ear before entering a small house, not far from the fire.

This sends me running out of the café to a nearby wall to calm down, Daniel follows behind, 'What's wrong lovely?' He asks all worried.

Still out of breath, I manage to answer, 'In another life we were I think brother and sister, when the last battle occurred, just over five-hundred years ago, we were,' I can hardly believe it myself, 'but that was then, not now.'

'Strange, perhaps there is a strong bond between us in the past that binds us together now?' He enquires.

'Possibly,' I sigh, 'time will tell.'

Chapter 19 - Headed into the loft, the ball is rolling

For a few days now I'd felt a dark cloud hanging over me, other little things were concerning me, things like - where would I live? Would I have a place of my own? Or would I be burdening my family due living with them?

Arriving through my front door, didn't feel quite the same, I wasn't sure as to why.

After a short break, I start to read, trying hard to forget the daunting task that lay ahead.

Later in the day, despite putting it off, it was time to go into the loft, to sort through everything that was up there. My parents, lives were up there, hidden inside those boxes - photos, letters, clothes and somewhere in one of the boxes, their wedding rings.

Passing Gabriel on the stairs, my heart heavy and my mind consumed.

He grabs hold of my hand, 'What's wrong my love?'

'So much sorrow, so much to sort and so much to let go of,' a deep breath, 'yet much to look forward to,' I kiss his forehead, 'if you need me, I'll be in the loft.'

In the loft, I feel as if time has stood still, that within each box is a piece of my parent's history, 'May as well start at the back, could be here a while.' I chuckle quietly to myself.

A silver box catches my eye, as I open the box, my fingers tremble. Wave after wave of laughter escapes my lips; the silver box is filled with photos of me when I was young, looking at one photo in particular stops me in my tracks, – it was my thirteenth birthday, I was dressed in jeans, trainers and a gypsy top, at either side of me were my parents, beaming happily, my face is all scrunched up, about to blow out the candles on the cake, taking care my hair didn't accidentally set fire. Ah, the time of innocence.

By 6:00pm, half the boxes were sorted, in that time I'd had an idea - keep what I wanted and give the rest to the local museum, they were always lacking old photos, costumes, etc.

Some of the boxes contained jewellery that must have been 300yrs old, maybe even older, other boxes contained; clothes, photos, postcards and letters that my mother and father had written to each other long ago.

Cold hands caught my hips as I descended the ladder, spinning around it was Michael, 'I have something for you.' I smile whilst reaching into my pocket, a special photograph; of him and my parents, they all looked so happy.

His eyes glazed over, in response I wrap my arms around him and kiss his cheek.

'Thankyou sweet Lydia, this photograph holds a lot of pride and admiration, this photo, I will treasure for eternity.'

Letting go I ask, 'Was the photo a turning point in your life? You look as if a huge weight had been lifted from your shoulders.'

'It was a time of great change and those two angels made a huge difference in my life, they made me realise I wasn't a monster.'

My eyes became moist, mainly with happiness that they had found a deep and lasting friendship.

I find Gabriel downstairs sitting on the sofa, sitting next to him I whisper, 'Sorry for being rude earlier.'

'I understand my love.' He rubs my hand gently before kissing it.

After tea I took a deep breath, 'Michael, can I have a word please? In the kitchen.'

Obliging, Michael steps into the kitchen and sits down opposite me.

'I'll need help filling out an application for a visa and work permit, where would I send it to?' I twiddle my fingers.

'No worries my dear,' slight pause, 'we can hand in the forms at the American embassy in London.'

Well, that was easy, 'Okay, what about living arrangements?'

'For a short while, you can live with us whilst we finish building you a house to call your own, we have plenty of land,' He sees the expression on my face, 'Lydia, everything will work out, just you wait and see, we will be with you every step of the way.'

His smile reassures me, 'Where do you live?'

'We live on the outskirts of Lancaster New Hampshire, Mount Washington isn't far away, it is located within the Presidential range of the white mountains. We are surrounded by hills, valleys and wide-open spaces,' another slight pause, 'all we need to know is; how many bedrooms you would like and such things as furnishings, bathrooms and decoration.'

Due to my excitement I blurted out - 'Three bedrooms would be brilliant, a space for a little library, two bathrooms and leave the rest to me.' I'd need Michael to arrange storage of my stuff until I arrived, will ask him later.

Walking into the front room Daniel and Gabriel looked bored, I decided we would all play cards to pass some time.

The sun began to rise by the time I settled into my bed and fell happily asleep.

Another week had flown by, Daniel was safely on his way home, I missed him dearly, but Daniel had given me his mobile number, he'd said just before going through the departure gates at the airport, 'Call me any time, hope to see you soon.' With that he'd waved and vanished.

I'd personally gone down to the American embassy in London to hand in my application for a visa.

I had also sorted things out with the local council, followed by a picnic by the river.

Walking towards the museum, my heart misses a beat, my mind alerts me to a possible fact I hadn't thought of – what if the museum didn't need these items? What would I do then? I couldn't burn them, nor could I take them with me. Taking a deep breath, I try to keep calm as I enter the museum. People seem to be rushing around, talking in hushed whispers, or musing over the museum's new little display.

Ringing the bell several times, an assistant finally arrives, 'Can I help you?'

'Is the manager available please? It's important.' I reply trying to keep the nerves from entering my voice.

'One moment please.' She replies.

She scuttles into the back room and after a moment she reappears, 'She will be straight down, just sorting out a bit of paperwork.' She smiles and takes a sip of her coffee.

'Thankyou.' I smile nervously.

Looking down at my feet, I'd brought five bags of things, mainly photos, clothes and some military items.

The manager arrives and gestures for me to follow her into an office down the hall, 'Hi I'm Caroline Scully, manager here.' She says as she closes the office door.

'Hi, I'm Lydia Chambers.'

'What can I do for you my dear?'

Sitting down on a chair I begin to nervously rub my knees, 'Well,' I swear I'm starting to sweat, 'Soon I'll be moving, and I've recently sorted out my loft,' I decide it would be easier to show her. I gently open all the bags one at a time, 'please take a peek, if anything is of use to the museum, you can have it.'

Her eyes lit up like Christmas lights, she stammers, 'Are you sure?'

I nod my head, 'Positive, I'll be moving, and I don't want to take everything with me, though sometimes I wish I could.' I feign a weak smile.

'All of these items will be most useful for various exhibitions and we will look after them, promise.'

Hiding what I had been doing, I hand her a cheque, 'To help with costs and maybe even a redecoration?' My heart lifts, just a little.

Caroline looks as if she is ready to pass out, I could hear her heartbeat thundering like a river in my ears. She stutters but can't manage a full sentence. My cue to go.

'Excuse me, I gotta go, still much left for me to do, I will send you my forwarding address, so you can keep me up to date on developments.' I quickly shake her hand, smile and walk out.

Outside on the street I inhale a deep breath, 'That went well.' I chuckle.

Wandering around the local park (it was a huge park with fountains, a bandstand, a small-scale railway you could sit on and ride and plenty of trees and green space.) felt peaceful and invigorating. Finding the perfect spot, I sit on an empty bench under the shade of a large old tree; couples were holding hands chattering, others were admiring the views and a few noisy people were shouting down their mobile phones, obviously unaware the whole park could hear them. This is bliss, peace, only Gabriel was missing, that would have made it perfect.

I start to run, slow and steady at first, until I was out of sight, it was then I picked up some speed, by the time I reach my front door I feel slightly out of breath yet energised.

'Good afternoon my love.' Gabriel calls.

I blow him a kiss and duck inside to make a brew.

Night time approached, as ever I wanted a bit of me time, I insisted they go on a hunt, since it had been a fortnight since their last hunt. Playfully I shove them out of the front door, promising to ring them if anything happens. Closing the door, I make soup, read a little before laying on the sofa.

'Such a manic time and still I knew that more tears would flow.' I say to myself as I find my page in the book.

Chapter 20 - **Time moves on, farewell and the home straight**

The past nine days had flown, most of them were spent touring the world.

Firstly, we flew over to Dublin and took a tour of the famous Guinness factory, I even sampled (again) their famous stout. For the night, we stayed in a hotel overlooking the river.

Early hours, we were up and off, this time to fly to Edinburgh, Gabriel had arranged a two-night stay in a hotel and a tour around the castle.

Soon as I arrived, I managed to find a ghost tour that was happening the following evening, without hesitation, I booked a ticket.

I leaned my head against the castle wall and closed my eyes. Hushed whispers and voices of people long ago fluttered through my mind, Gabriel's hand brought me round, 'Are you okay?'

'I'm fine, soaking up the atmosphere.' I smiled as we ducked indoors, just as the rain came down in buckets.

Somehow, it felt strange looking through someone else's former residence, after a few moments, that feeling melted away leaving me feeling relaxed.

Early evening and I was eating dinner in the local pub, 'Oh, this food is heavenly.' I smile happily shoving mouthful after mouthful in. I was almost certain I could eat them out of house and home.

I spent most of the night admiring the view from a big bay window, by the time I crept into bed, it wouldn't be long before I was up again.

The final night in Scotland was spent on a ghost tour, I'd never realised that under the streets of the city were underground streets, houses and even pubs. A few of the places gave me the creeps and was glad to be back out in the fresh night air.

I couldn't believe Michael and Gabriel, they had both been secretive as to our next location, so much so, they'd blindfolded me and made me wear earplugs until we had boarded the plane.

'Thanks for that.' I say semi-sarcastically.

'It's a surprise, I know you will love it and, I am going to spoil you rotten.' Gabriel replies with a devious grin.

To my eternal shock, we had landed in Italy, five days visiting various places.

'I will get you both for this one day.' The smile spreads across my face, I let out a squeal!

We spent time in Venice, Milan, Rome and Florence. Gabriel stuck to his word, he spoilt me rotten.

Before I knew it, it was time for us to fly back to England and I remembered that when we returned, they would only have two days left before they were due to fly home to the States.

Floods of panic washed over me, I spent most of the flight pulling more turbulence than the plane, constantly up and down, I needed to calm down.

Dawn came, and I was wide awake, today is the day I have to say a temporary goodbye to the love of my life and the man my parents adored.

All bags were packed and by the front door. I offered to drive them to the airport.

'It would be most gracious of you to drive us to the airport dear Lydia.'

'Well, saves your baggage flying out of the cases as you run.' I couldn't stop laughing at the images that conjured up, even Gabriel managed to crack one of his hypnotic smiles.

Just as we leave the house, the postie brings the mail, 'Thanks.'

He waves and wanders back to his van.

'Will take a quick look, then I'll hop into the driver's seat.' I wink.

I chuck the usual mail in the house; one letter stands out. Cautiously opening it I see the letter head, pulling out the entire letter; I read it with excitement running through my veins, 'Yes, yes yes, I've been accepted, I can come, yippee.'

Both vampires in the car laugh and smile, in Gabriel's eyes I can see relief.

'Okay time to go.' I say as I lock the front door.

Arriving at the airport, it was busy as usual. I helped grab the bags and suitcases from the boot, then leaned against the car, this is the moment of truth, no tears until they were out of sight.

Michael hugged me, 'See you soon,' quick pause, 'will leave you two alone for a few moments.' With that he walked into the airport entrance.

'So,' I mumble, 'this is it for a while.'

Gabriel ran his fingers through my hair, and pressed my head against his rippled chest, 'I don't want to go.' He whimpered.

I made him look me in the eye, 'You have to go and anyway it won't be long before I join you.' I try to smile.

He growled, 'How can you stand this?'

'Because I know you will always be with me, no matter how far the distance.' That came straight from the heart.

Gabriel let go, 'You really are a one off,' change of subject, 'I best go, but I will ring you soon as we return home and each night until you are in my arms again.'

He nuzzles into my chest one last time, to hear my heart beating strong, it was then he slowly walks away. I wave until they are both out of sight.

Climbing back into the car, I let one tear slip, looking down I spy a small package with my name on, opening it, I see the most gorgeous pendant staring back at me. Underneath it was a simple note saying, "*Because of you, always and forever.*'

The pendant was that of a vampire freely holding his heart to the sky, the heart had tiny wings.

Tears sprung forth, after composing myself I set off, heading for home.

Six weeks had passed since the farewells at the airport, just four more weeks to go before the start of my new life in a new country.

I spoke to Gabriel each night, usually until the early hours of the morning. I missed him being here with me.

Most of my belongings had already been put into storage until my arrival, Michael had told me that my new place of residence was half built. Slowly but surely excitement grew.

The bank etc. had been notified of my move, so the majority of the hard work was out of the way, as we all know the hardest job is saying goodbye to everything we know and, saying goodbye to loved ones who had gone to heaven. In a weird sense, my parents had already left me, but in my mind, memories burnt ferociously.

I'm making my way to the cemetery to visit my parents grave, I have new plants to place there and news to tell them.

Questions began swirling through my mind - who would look after the grave? Who would renew the plants each year? And could I really leave them behind?

Kneeling down at their graveside I make a silent promise, 'Once a year, I will come and make sure things are okay.' With that I open my eyes, as the sky grows overcast.

I sit at the side of them and begin talking, 'Hope I like Lancaster,' deep breath, 'I'll be protected, sounds like a silly thing,' I breathe a sigh of relief, 'choice requires sacrifice.'

Beaming proudly, I tidy up the headstone, plant the new plants, chat for a while before I turn my back and make my way home.

Instead of cooking I order takeaway, a whole feast fit for four people, all for me, believe me, I need the energy.

My parents bed was already in storage, wardrobes, drawers etc. had been taken by a charity, some of their clothes had gone into storage too, the rest went to a local theatre company.

Eating my takeaway in a quiet house made me feel slightly uneasy, the land line rings, 'Hello.'

'Hi love, it's me.' Gabriel's voice replies.

My brain begins to melt into my heart, even the sound of his voice can reduce me to mush in under a second, 'How're you? Enjoying home?'

'Missing you, home feels lonely, how are you my lovely?' He sighs.

His velvet voice still echoes in my ear, 'Much the same, trying to keep busy, sorting, eating and missing you.'

'You sound tired sweetheart.' Concern taints his reply.

'Lately, I haven't been sleeping well, I'm sure it'll pass.' my gut instinct springs to life, 'have you hunted recently?'

'I'll be fine.' He replies.

I blow a little raspberry, 'Enjoy yourself, go and hunt.' I shove a piece of chicken in my mouth.

'Okay, if you insist,' He sighs heavily, 'I cannot wait until you are safely in my arms.'

Shit! I'm starting to blush, 'Love you forever, will speak to you in a few days' time.'

'I love you, more than you will ever know, always and forever.' He says in his perfect velvet voice.

'Goodbye.' I smile and put the phone down.

Ah, my few moments of bliss each night. Time for more food.

Chapter 21 - Tears, tantrums and goodbye England, hello New Hampshire

Only seven days remain, seven days until I leave this house, my old life and the only country I know. Hell, I'm scared to death!

Just gone midnight, I run out of the house and up to the woods, I wanted to stay a while with my old friend – the gnarled oak tree. The tree had been a part of my entire life and I wanted to say goodbye.

Fog quickly enveloped the woods, wrapping itself around the trees and weaving itself amongst the night air.

'Hello old friend,' I whisper to the tree, I run my finger against the marking I made so many years ago, 'you always listen, without judgement and condemnation,' I light up a cigarette, 'I've come to say that shortly, I'll be leaving, to start what I hope will be an adventurous new life, thousands of miles away,' the tree gently creaks, 'I will come and visit, you hold so much of my childhood in your branches,' I giggle, 'I remember when I first climbed you, took me hours to figure out how to get down again.'

With that memory replaying in my mind, I hug the oak tree, sit down beneath its sturdy branches and allow my memories to take me back in time.

A day to go until I go to the hotel near the airport, my flight is the day after that. My heart thunders, almost in desperation, kicking my suitcase, I sit on the floor with my legs crossed, 'You need this,' I scold myself, 'just this once, you deserve this, and I owe it to myself to take this step.' My voice echoes round the empty room.

It's time to ring Gabriel, I feel in a pickle, 'Damn, it's engaged, I'll try again in a minute.'

A few minutes pass, I try again.

'Hello.' Says a strange voice.

I gulp audibly, 'Is Gabriel there please?'

'Hold on.' The male voice replies.

'Hey gorgeous.' Gabriel addresses me in his husky tone.

I suppress a fit of laughter, 'Hi lovely, just wanted to hear your voice.'

'Is something wrong?'

Sighing, 'Nerves I guess, I'm sure it'll pass.'

'Awe, you sweet little thing, it will work out, I promise.'

It is always easier said than done, I trust things happen for a reason, 'Will ring you on the morning of the flight, you can fill me in on the details such as, who's picking me up.'

'Of course, goodbye beautiful, I love you.' His voice echoed.

Not again, my cheeks are burning, 'Goodbye love of my life, I love you too.'

Now to waste some time, before jumping in the car to get takeaway.

My house keys drop to the floor, 'Fuck sake.'

The taxi driver pips his horn, he's only just pulled up, I yell 'Alright, I'm coming, god damn it.' I stub my foot on the gatepost.

Shoving my suitcase in the back, I hop into the front, 'There, happy now?' I stare right at him.

'Why shout at me?'

'You pipped your horn, it wasn't necessary.' I exhale.

The driver uses a softer tone, 'You're about to spread those wings, I remember when I first moved out.' He smiles, putting the car in gear.

I smile a little, 'Does it get easier?'

'With time, yes.'

The taxi begins to draw away from the house, tears are already streaming down my face.

A little way further down the road, we pass the cemetery and the tears come thick and fast. The driver hands me a tissue, 'Thanks.' I try to console myself.

Pulling up outside the hotel, I look bleary eyed and feel exhausted.

'How may I help you?' The assistant behind the desk asks.

'Reservation for Chambers.' I feel ready to collapse.

'Ah, yes, room nine, first floor, sign this please, then I can hand over the keys.'

I sign the piece of paper, hand it back and he hands me the key.

'Have a nice stay.'

'Thanks.' I try to smile, 'which way do I go?'

He goes red, 'Turn left at the end of the hall, take the lift to the first floor, when you get out, turn right and it is the first door on the left.'

'Cheers.' I wearily drag myself down the hall towards the lift.

Plonking my suitcase down, I lay on the huge bed staring at the ceiling decoration, 'Interesting.' I mutter.

After a while and faking a smile, the reflection didn't lie, there was still hurt and pain within me, if you looked beyond the red rimmed eyes and into my soul, there was a void that (at this present time) felt endless. Time to venture out and find somewhere to eat.

10:00pm, just got back to the hotel, a quick shower, relax listening to some music, then sleep.

If I get to sleep.

7:00am, Friday, I'm awake, frantically packing, making sure I'm not leaving things behind.

Funny thing is - my flight isn't for twelve hours. Time to kill I guess.

Okay, best finalise the details with Gabriel, last thing I need is to cock up.

'It's the middle of the night.' Gabriel laughs.

Bouncing onto the bed, 'You're a vampire, you don't sleep.' I can't stop laughing.

'What's up sweetie?'

'Remember, we need to iron out details.'

'Of course,' pause, 'I'll be there at Newark to pick you up,' sighing, 'to hold my one true love, ah truly I will soon have everything I could dream of.'

'I can't wait to feel your arms lovingly around me,' back to the subject at hand, 'Is anyone else gonna be there?' And how much progress has been made on the house?'

'Haven't decided yet, as for your house, it is two weeks from completion.'

'My house? Don't you mean our house? Or am I living alone?' I feel confused.

'Sorry my love, I didn't mean to alarm you, of course we shall be living together, at last.'

Gabriel growls softly, the type of growl that sends shivers of delight down my spine.

'Sorry to have disturbed you." I reply meekly.

'Honey, have no worries, I could listen to your voice forever, all that is missing is your heart beating against my chest.'

A single tear of happiness runs softly down my cheek, 'I love you so much, much more than I could ever say.'

'And my sweetheart, you are the one for me,' He chuckles darkly, 'wait until I get you home.'

I smile with delight, 'I have to go, things to do, I'll see you outside Newark airport, I'll ring you before I head outside.'

'Goodbye beautiful.'

'Bye.' I end the call, lay upon the bed and smile.

I'd paid extra, so I could check out this afternoon, staring out of the window, the city is coming to life. The scent of fresh bread fills my nostrils and taunts my taste buds, 'Time to take a walk.'

My final day in England, my final day in the country I will forever call home.

Oh my god, this is heaven – bacon butty, huge mug of tea and one massive egg custard.

The assistant is watching me in amazement, as I wolf down all these delights in quick succession, 'My last day in England,' I say before guzzling the last of my brew, 'another please.'

Maybe my body will pay me back later? Who cares, I'm enjoying these delights.

5:00pm, check in had opened and I was first in line. Showing the check in lady my passport, flight ticket etc. I will have some time to kill before boarding. Dragging my luggage, I head for a restaurant to order some food and watch time slip away.

My entire body shakes as I climb the stairs to the aero plane, turning around I wave to no-one, turn back, enter the plane and find my seat.

A stewardess is going to look after me for a while, until I feel more settled. She's got the most gorgeous smile, 'You have a fantastic smile.'

'Awe, why thank you ma'am.' She replies.

'Please, call me Lydia.'

'Hi Lydia, my name is Cass,' smiling, 'I'll be back to check on you soon.' Cass stands up.

'Yeah sure, other people to look after.' I watch Cass walk down the aisle.

A short time later and the plane slowly lifts off into the air, looking out of the window I whisper, 'Goodbye.'

Rubber screeches on tarmac at one of Newark's runways.

A tingly sensation runs down my spine as the plane comes to a gradual standstill.

I go through customs without much difficulty, I even declare I was glad to be here and couldn't stop laughing, now time to go wait for my luggage.

After collecting my luggage, I was taking my first few steps into a new city. Stepping outside, I could see that it was dusk, but this bustling city seemed to be coming to life. Looking to my right, I spy a familiar face, blood rushes to my cheeks, my heart beats so quick, I wonder if I'm going to pass out? Two more familiar outlines appear from the shadows of a tree, my nerves take over, laughing my head off, crying with happiness and shaking like a leaf, I leap into Gabriel's arms, 'At last.' I kiss his neck.

He places me down and rests his ear to my chest and begins growling softly, 'My love.'

'Love birds,' Daniel pipes up, 'enough, it can wait.' He smiles.

I run to him, slap him on the shoulder, followed by a massive hug, 'Nice to see you.'

'I missed you too,' He clears his throat, 'too much mushy, c'mon, time to head home.'

Michael picks up my suitcases, places them in the boot of the car and shakes my hand.

As I'm getting into the car, something makes me feel instantly uneasy, getting out, I look across the street to see a strange woman staring at me as she leans against a mini cooper.

Gabriel grabs me and gently gets me inside the car, 'Anything wrong love?'

I lie, 'No, nothing,' changing subject, 'time to head for home.'

The engine roars to life, and as we pull away, I can't shake the bad feeling building inside me.

Chapter 22 - **New home and shocks**.

Fresh paint clung to the air, opening the windows, I'm hoping the smell goes away by the end of today. I feel at home, the front room is huge, one wall is dedicated to my family photos, the rest have little oil paintings on or pictures of dragons and wolves. Bright oak polished floors reflect light, the bookcase, sofa and other things fit nicely. A handmade rug finishes off the lounge perfectly.

Every room is oversized, including the bathroom and small library at the top of the house.

I'm lounging on the sofa reading a book, still in awe of my new surroundings. I've been here just over a month.

At the end of the first week, Gabriel said he had a surprise for me and it was waiting in the garage. Being blind folded was not the easiest thing for me.

'Okay you can take the blindfold off now love.' Gabriel gently let go of me, allowing me to take the infernal thing off.

'Oh fuck,' I holler, my eyes felt as if they had just done the popping out on stalks thing, you know the kind of thing you see on T.V. 'are you bloody serious?'

'You need a decent set of wheels.' Daniel smiles.

'Especially since you live out here.' Michael confirms.

In fact, there were two vehicles, both for me. One was a dodge RAM, black in colour.

However, it was the other car that made my eyes stand out on stalks – A limited edition Ford GT40, silver with two stripes down the centre of the car.

'Truly, I'm been spoilt rotten.'

Above the tempest, in the early hours of Saturday; I can hear my heart thundering, looking out of the window, it is pitch black, until, for a second, the lightning lights up the sky, illuminating the blackness, 'Time to venture out, can't miss this.' With that I grab my coat, put on my wellies and step out into the raging storm.

I never noticed Gabriel was stood behind me, until I turn around and nearly jump out of my skin, 'Gee, thanks.' I put my hand on my chest.

'Sorry love,' he wraps an arm around me, 'thought you would be asleep?'

'And miss this?' I smile, 'is something wrong?' He seemed tense.

'Someone is visiting, she will be here later.' His dark mood annoys me.

'Oh, okay,' I won't push any further, instead I decide to head indoors and make a hot chocolate, 'you coming in?' I gesture.

'Of course.' His arm is tightly wrapped round my waist as we head inside.

8:00am, I'm happily soaking in the bath, pondering why Gabriel seems so uptight about a visitor. All I know is – her name is Anna-Maria and she is Michael's niece.

Coming out of the bathroom, I see Gabriel staring at me hungrily, 'Yes.' I enquire innocently.

He raises one eyebrow, 'Tempting.' He growls.

Before I can answer he sweeps me off my feet, takes me into the bedroom and closes the door.

'Wow,' I think to myself, 'what a morning.' I'm in a daze as we enter the Hanson household.

Although Gabriel smiles, tension is written all over his features, as a car pulls up.

Michael had told her that I was now living here and that I was safe. What a way to start, I sound more important when all I am is human.

A tall woman with striking green eyes steps out of the mini cooper.

I whisper to Gabriel, 'She's the one I saw across the road, when you picked me up from Newark.'

He tightens his protective grip around me.

Anna is taller than me, with sweeping long hair, a bright smile, she is wearing; jeans, hiking boots and a chunky jumper, still that didn't stop her looking like a mega star.

There's friction between her and Gabriel, I can see it, she hugs Michael, Alison and Callum, but walks straight past Gabe towards me, 'Oh dear hell.' I think.

She extends her hand, 'Hi Lydia, I'm Anna-Maria.'

I gulp loudly and extend my hand, 'Hi, pleased to meet you.'

Anna-Maria steps back and heads towards the kitchen, something deep within me stirred, it warned me to be wary of her.

Her skin was warm and her grip strong. Perhaps she wasn't all vampire?

Not long after Anna had left, for some unknown reason; I gave Gabriel a kiss on the cheek and whispered, 'Broken.' followed by touching his chest and walking out of the house.

'Where the hell did that come from?' I scold myself as I close the front door of the Hanson house.

I jumped onto the roof of my house and gazed at the sun. Why had I said it? What motivated me to say it? My instincts were telling me I was right, that Gabriel has or had a broken heart, even though it stopped beating long ago.

'What the-.' I managed to mumble as I slide off the roof.

A strong hand grabbed me and pulled me back to the spot I was sitting not a moment before.

Looking around, it was Daniel, slapping him hard I growl with shock, 'Don't ever do that, ever again.' Damn, I forgot he was coming, how much time had passed?

'Sorry,' He gave me his best puppy dog eyes, 'why you up here?'

'To clear my mind,' I'm sounding confused, 'I said something to Gabe, but the thing is, it came out of no-where.'

Daniel becomes suspicious, 'You two had a fight?'

'No,' my voice is barely a whisper, 'I put my hand on his heart and said it was broken.'

He smiles, 'Maybe it was,' He hugs me, 'but now it is more alive than ever, I've seen the transformation,' kissing my forehead, 'you made that possible.'

'Don't paint me as a saint,' standing up, 'I'm only human,' turning around, 'ready to have an afternoon of fun?'

'Sure, let's go.'

I jump off the roof and head into Lancaster with Daniel.

Sat in the early evening air, Daniel has just left, which doesn't give me much time to try and explain to Gabe about my sudden and unprovoked outburst.

Looks like I'm out of time, Gabriel is stepping out of the Hanson household and headed this way.

'Good evening.' I mumble as I get to my feet.

Gabriel towers over me, 'Oh, how I missed you my love.'

I kiss his hand, 'I'm so sorry about my outburst earlier today.'

Gabriel replies huskily, 'You were right,' He smiles, 'about my heart being broken,' his lips brush against mine, 'but guess what?'

Tingling runs up and down my spine, the tip of my tongue brushes the corner of his mouth, 'What?' I pant, almost in anticipation.

'You saved me from an eternity in darkness,' his hand plays gently with my neck, his other hand places my hand on his chest, where his heart is located, 'broken no longer, all thanks to you.'

A tear slid down my cheek and I kiss him full force on the lips, 'I love you.'

Gabe growls softly from his throat, 'I love you, I would die for you.'

Chapter 23 - **Getting lost and hiking, with bears?**

'Oh God,' I gulp, 'first day at work tomorrow,' shaking hands, 'I'm scared.' Looking in the mirror, my entire body begins to shake with nerves.

Luckily, Michael works there too, so I will be following him in my car tomorrow.

Time for a bike ride through the woods, lots of obstacles for me to manoeuvre around, the ride may even clear my mind.

Although the wind feels harsh, it doesn't really bother me, what is bothering me however was this - someone is following me on my ride, one whiff and I knew instantly who it was - Gabriel. A smile spreads across my face, bringing the bike to a sudden halt, I turn, 'No need to follow.'

A voice echoes, 'I like to watch you, you're such a fascinating creature.'

Laughing loudly, I shout, 'Keep up.'

My legs push the pedals faster and faster, weaving in and out of the trees. The pace is exhilarating, the wind begins to pick up, but that only spurs me to go faster, dodging trees and going down some of the steepest terrain I had known.

Evening arrives in this vast open land, while my homemade soup gently simmers on the hob, I step outside to watch night creep across Mount Washington. Callum is standing on the porch of the Hanson household, 'Evening.' I call.

'Hey.' Callum calls back as he walks over towards me.

'How are you Callum?' I ask.

'Not bad thank you, how are you? Settling in okay?'

'I guess so,' sitting on a step, 'just nerves catching up on me, soon as tomorrow is over, I'll be okay.'

Callum intrigued me, he was a few inches taller than me, with sandy brown hair and a smile that would dazzle a lion.

'It does take time, but it will be worth it,' He smiles again, 'goodnight.' He wanders back to the Hanson house.

Been alone doesn't bother me as much as it used to, loneliness no longer made my heart sink and make me dread-

'Evening sweetheart.' His voice purrs.

Standing up I turn to face him, in the fading light he looks more spectacular than I realised, the thoughts running in my mind have me frozen to the spot with a grin on my face.

'Honey, are you okay?' Gabriel snaps his fingers in front of me.

Although I see the action, my thoughts still have me frozen in time, I manage to mumble, 'Pardon?'

Damn, snap out of it, shaking my head the thoughts trickle out and I tuck my tongue back in my mouth.

'I asked if you were okay.' He repeats.

'Yes, perfectly thanks.' I smile awkwardly.

'You were staring at me, almost as if it was the first time you saw me.'

Damn, he's good, 'The fading light, your features, dirty thoughts.' I don't know if to laugh or cry.

By the look on Gabriel's face, he wonders if I'm serious? All of a sudden, his face lights up, a wicked smile spreads across his face, he growls in my ear, puts his hands on my hips. Shit! He's sending my senses all over the place. Out of impulse I kiss him, slowly and deliberately, my fingertips gently trace his spine.

Gabriel growls as his lips push onto mine, locking eyes we're not sure where this will take us.

Slowly I back off, 'That's just a taster,' I raise and lower my eyebrow, 'right now I need food.'

Kissing him on the tip of his nose, I do a little wiggle as I walk into the house.

6:00am, showered and dressed, sitting downstairs drinking a hot chocolate. Gabriel's thumb is rubbing gently against my knuckles, to calm me down.

'You'll be fine love.' He reassures me.

'I hope so.' I reply.

Just gone 7:00am, I'm sat in my car, waiting for Michael, he is going to show me the way, he will be home before I am.

As we both pull into the General practice car-park, I again realise the responsibility resting upon my shoulders.

'Have a good day, see you this evening.' I call over to Michael.

In the blink of an eye he is giving me a hug, 'You'll have a fantastic first day, see you back home this evening.'

Michael kisses me on the cheek and vanishes inside the building, I, however, light up a cigarette to calm my nerves.

The sun begins to set and guess what? I'm lost, 'Damn it,' I growl, 'how the hell did I get lost?'

Pulling over, I decide to look at a map, not that I'm any good with map reading. I'm not ringing anyone until I figure this out. Shit, the battery on my phone is dead, so that throws my emergency call out of the way.

It is almost dark out, I'm here, trying to figure out where the hell I am.

From somewhere outside, a branch snaps, jumping out of my skin I dive onto the back seat, praying like hell. For some reason, I start to hear whispers, the voices are incomprehensible, just mutters and echoes carried by the wind.

'Okay girl, you need to man up and see who, or what is out there.'

Getting my shakes under control, I shimmy across and push the door slowly outwards. I crawl onto the floor and stand bolt upright, scanning the surroundings for possible threats.

Nothing, absolutely nothing- the scent of diesel fills my nostrils, 'No, it can't be the tank leaking,' grabbing a torch, I aim it at the tank, only to see no leaks, 'phew.' I wipe my forehead.

I'm puzzled as to where the smell is coming from, looking South I see a small petrol station, into the boot I go, grab a huge plastic can and race down the road, purse in my mouth.

Happily, I skip back to the dodge, fill up the tank, jump in the car, rev the engine, oh how I love the growl of the engine, putting it in gear and with a hand drawn map by one of the attendants, I head back home.

'Hiking?' I wail, 'Hiking? Why?' I wail again.

Daniel is laughing at my outcry.

'I'm not good with hiking, I'm accident prone.'

'We're going hunting,' Michael says, 'why are you against hiking?'

'Coz, I can't climb, I fall over my own feet and who's gonna look after me?'

Staring at the entire room, my question had stumped them, guess they weren't expecting that.

Gabriel sits next to me, 'Love, come with us, just once,' sighing, 'I know you can look after yourself.'

Damn, suppose he's right, 'Okay okay, best go buy some hiking boots and waterproofs.'

I can't help but chuckle as visions of myself falling into streams run through my mind.

5:00am, all ready to go, food packed into a bag along with other essentials. On the horizon is – White Mountain national forest, 'Okay let's do this, before I change my mind.' I grumble.

Gabriel grabs hold of my hand and away we go, I can hardly feel the weight of the bag on my back as we race further and further away from home.

The expanse of land before us was heavily coated in snow and ice.

'Is this Canada?' I enquire.

'It is my love,' smelling the air, 'you best go somewhere safe sweetheart, I know where to find you.' He smiles.

'Okay,' kissing his cheek, 'see ya later.'

I take a few steps back, Anna stands there, admiring the view.

In an instant they were gone, chasing down their prey.

Anna smiles, 'Shall we?' She points in the direction where the gang sped off towards.

'How?' Raising my eyebrows.

Anna smirks and points, 'In those woods about twenty miles away, we can stay high, you'll be safer up high, especially to sleep.'

I'm such a novice, 'Let's go.'

After a few slips and slides we arrive in the woods and the temperature is dropping rapidly, time to make a fire.

Anna sets up the tent, it is somewhere to shelter for a while.

With the fire going, I warm up some soup, Anna sits opposite me, she stares at me, which gives me shivers, 'Yes?'

'Not bad, for a novice.'

It is pitch black, apart from the small amount of light given off by the dying embers of the fire, my eyes are beginning to droop, Anna nudges me, 'Sleepy head.' She whispers.

'I know, I know, time to crawl in the tent, don't think I can make it up into the trees.'

We both scoot into the tent, I crawl into my sleeping bag, before I know it, my eyes close as sleep takes over.

Saturday afternoon and I'm practising climbing trees as fast as possible, without falling down. So far 50/50 success. Well at least my audience seems entertained.

'Try and see where you are going to put your feet, before you make the climb.' Callum shouts.

'At this rate, there won't be anything left of me.' I shout back, half laughing.

Jumping down, I stare long and hard at the tree. I see places I can place my feet, with my new-found knowledge, I put it to the test. My eyes scan for the next hand or foot hold, at last I make it up, 'How long did I take?'

'Eight seconds,' Michael calls out, 'well done.'

Now I understood, for next time.

Jumping down from the tree, I hug Gabriel, 'I could stay like this forever.'

'And so could I my sweet Lydia,' His arms wrap around me, 'so could I.'

It's the middle of the night, the wind is whipping the tent into a frenzy, I'm sitting in a corner with my sleeping bag and plenty of layers on. In the middle of the tent is my wind-up torch; casting strange shadows all around, Anna is happily reading a book, not phased one bit by the weather conditions.

'Calm down,' Anna giggles, 'the wind can't hurt you.'

'I'm trying, really I-'

Above the wind, we both pick up a new sound and it doesn't sound happy.

'What the hell is that?' I think to myself.

Crawling out of my sleeping bag and out of the tent, despite the wind blurring my vision, an unmistakable shape comes into my line of sight, 'BEAR!!!!' I shout.

Anna comes rushing out, 'Shit,' She growls, 'run, run, RUN!' She shouts at the top of her lungs.

Scrambling off the floor, we both make a run for it. The Bear is catching up and is growling furiously.

'Now what?' Anna yells to Lydia.

'Keep running, we either out run it, or turn and-'

It was too late, the Bear had caught up with me, 'Fuck, fuck, fuck.' I curse as the bear knocks me sideways.

I land hard on compacted snow, the bear tries to pin me to the floor, I have one small window of opportunity and I take it. With one swift kick I manage to kick the bear, he roars in pain, I try to crawl away from the immediate danger. Scrambling to get onto my knees, I crawl backwards, again the bear comes at me, fury and confusion in his eyes, then all of a sudden; the bear looks to be flying away from me, as if he's been tossed into the air.

Laying on the snow I puff and pant, 'That was close.'

My entire body aches and confusion sets in.

I hear voices, 'Lydia.' the voices call, and people come closer.

Anna had brought reinforcements in the form of Gabriel and Callum.

'So that's how the bear was able to fly.' I laugh and find I'm out of breath yet again.

Gabriel's face is an inch away from my own, 'Lydia, love are you alright?' His voice is filled with panic.

'I think so,' I spat out breathlessly, 'is it time for home?'

Gabriel kisses my forehead, 'We are, just waiting for Michael and Allison,' between kisses, 'I'll stay with you.'

I breathe a sigh of relief, shortly we will be heading home.

Chapter 24 - **Disagreement and Christmas shopping**.

Christmas isn't far away, twenty-four days to be exact. In recent years, Christmas meant misery, pain and loneliness, because my parents are no longer here.

This year will be different, I'm surrounded by family and my first of many here in America.

'Oh bollocks,' I mumble, 'what do vampires do this time of year?'

I'd have to hold that thought until later, my next patient is due any minute.

The day has ended, and I'm homeward bound, on foot. It's dark and a thick fog is descending. For once my mind is clear but my body is exhausted, still I carry on walking home.

Ah, the night feels like a long-forgotten friend, night time had always offered me an escape, it had hidden me from the world and made me feel secure in the knowledge that - nothing lasts forever.

Yes, home is in sight, running to the front door, I race in and collapse on the sofa.

A pair of cool arms lift me off the sofa, soft lips caress mine.

'Hello sleepy.' He whispers in my ear.

The air escapes my lungs, breathing out a sigh of relief, 'Hi.' I'm still not quite awake.

Gabriel places me on my bed and lays next to me, smiling.

'What do you all do for Christmas?'

A look of delight crosses his face, as he thinks about the answer, the house is still, waiting in baited breath for his answer.

'We usually go on a big hunt, starting Christmas eve, followed by exchanging presents on New Year's Eve.'

I nearly choke, 'Wow,' composing myself, 'Well, at least I'm working Christmas eve.'

Looks like I'll be spending Christmas alone. I let out a long sigh.

'Michael has already discussed this with us,' smiling, 'Christmas dinner at Michaels, Daniel, Anna-Maria and others will be there, we shall go hunting on the 23rd and return late on the 24th,' looking into Lydia's eyes, 'did you think we would leave you alone for Christmas?'

'I guess so,' stretching, 'but I was prepared for that.'

Gabriel kisses my hand, 'How could we leave you here? It simply would not be fair on you.'

'I'm used to a life that isn't fair,' I smile weakly, 'I've been given the best gift of all, something greater than life itself.'

'What is that then?' He asks curiously.

Looking deep into his eyes, 'A love I thought I'd never find.' I pressed my lips against his chest, at the place where his heart would have been beating furiously.

A soft growl echoed up, escaping his lips. Instantly his fingers were roaming softly through my hair.

Gabriel pulled me against him, 'I want you, so much.'

Before a sound escapes my lips, he pins me to the bed and presses his marble like body against mine, 'You are mine.' He whispers huskily into my ear.

Ten tender fingers manage to slide out of his iron grip and gently dance over his body.

'Great,' I growl, looking out of my bedroom window, I see Anna-Maria's car pull up, 'just what I need on my day off, chaos.' Sighing heavily, I trudge towards my bed and slowly get dressed.

I had no clue as to why Anna-Maria gave me the creeps, or why she seemed to bring out the worst in me.

Plodding out of my house, I walk into the Hanson household and straight into trouble - Anna-Maria.
She stares at me with harsh eyes, as if I'm a pest that needs eliminating.
Instead of trying to pass her, I stare right back, in an instant I'm staring at a wall, 'Rude.' I curse under my breath.

From somewhere in the living room I hear her response, 'Moron.'

This will end up giving me a headache, sooner or later we will clash.

In the kitchen, I stare out of the window. Slowly turning around, my hands begin to shake and so does my voice.

'Battle-axe.' we both say at the same time, her eyes register shock, I remain silent, stunned by our choice of words.

Gabriel walks in and Anna storms out.

Without hesitation I open the largest kitchen window and fling myself out of it, landing on my feet I walk slowly away from the house.

Anger boils within me, I want to scream out the frustration, but there was simply no point.

I feel Gabriel's hands on my shoulders, turning around, I see doubt and anger cross his perfect face.

'Something ain't right.' I tell him straight.

'Like what love?' He questions back.

Looking directly at him, the answer flashes before my eyes, 'You and Anna were once an item, you thought she was the one, but it turned sour.' There is no emotion in my words.

Gabriel hangs his head and mumbles, 'Yes.'

I knew what I was about to say would sound selfish, I needed to know, I needed certainty, 'Is that what you'll do to me? Get rid of me because I'm not the one?' still I had more to say and although inside I trembled, tears ran down my cheeks, I point and shake my finger with fear, 'you're the one and only for me, if I'm not the one for you, I need to know, I refuse to spend eternity spitting out anger and rage like a volcano.'

I had always been insecure about relationships, I'd seen so many go wrong.

Gabriel holds his head high, his eyes glaze over and sorrow rests upon his features, regret, anger and belief linger in his angelic voice, 'She was not the other half of my soul, she did not fit with me,' he takes a step towards Lydia, 'you were the missing part, always, when I laid eyes upon you, I knew there and then you were the one,' another step closer, 'I could never hurt you,' one more step closer, 'look into my eyes.'

I lock eyes with his, for a moment I feel as if my heart stops beating, 'I had to know.' with a sharp intake of breath.

He swings his arm around my shoulder, 'Be assured, you are the love of my life, the one who consistently shows me the way, even in my darkest hour.'

He plants a kiss on my cheek. We spend some time in the woods.

Gabriel reveals his past relationship with Anna and how it turned out.

Six shopping days left until Christmas, a field day for Alison, I'm meeting her after work, I groan, 'This is gonna be hell.'

A sudden hot flush makes me switch on my desk fan, the cooling breeze is gentle, I need something harsher; opening the window, I inhale a lungful of winter air.

By dinnertime I felt worse, I'd got off the phone with Michael who suggested I take it easy and if necessary, go home early, to try get some rest before meeting Alison.

My phone rings, 'Hello.'

'Michael has phoned me, he says to take it easy with you as you are not feeling your usual self.'

It's Alison, breathing a sigh of relief, 'I keep going hot then cold, the winter air should do me some good, see you later?'

'I will meet you outside work in three hours, take it easy, bye.'

'Thanks, bye .' I lean back in my chair and stare at the ceiling.

Leaving work, the winter air smacks me in the face, I inhale the cold air through my mouth.

The taste of cinnamon is tingling on my tongue, 'Hi Alison.'

'Hello sister,' she smiles back, 'ready?'

'As ready as I'll ever be.' I manage a weak smile.

Getting into her car, we are ready to head off.

'What do I get Gabe?' I shout over to Alison.

As she is about to answer, my eyes came across a Celtic love knot bracelet, 'Perfect.' I smile.

Alison looks over my shoulder and looks approvingly.

By 2:00pm the Christmas present shopping was done, now the really evil part that I had been dreading - clothes shopping.

My fever was dying down, I quickly dive into a shop and buy a jumper. Its warmth is soothing, not suffocating like my fever.

Fifteen shopping bags later, we're heading back to the car, each item of clothing had been handpicked by Alison, though I did manage to sneak in some t-shirts and jeans.

Driving back, I had the window open fully and Alison kindly called off at a drive-thru so I could order food.

I dive right in, hunger fueling me on, Alison looked at me and began giggling.

Looking at her, food escaping my mouth with innocent eyes, quickly swallowing the food, I feel the fever is returning, Alison's eyes turn from fun to concerned.

I wave my hand, 'I'll be fine, just need to lay down for a bit.'

Instead of laying down, I wrapped presents, 'Why do I feel so ill?' I moan at the empty room.

After wrapping, I pushed on but by 9.30pm I lay shivering on the huge sofa.

Gabriel had done some research and had come up with nothing.

He was watching me as I lay on the sofa, I hated the fact he was concerned for me, he shouldn't have to feel that way.

'I'll be fine,' deep breath, 'probably just a bug.' I tried to reassure him but he was having none of it.

'You're a bad liar,' he says, 'it has to be something more,' worry tainted his voice, 'shall I stay with you tonight?'

It sounded more like he was going to stay with me, like it or not, 'Please.' I say sleepily.

He carries me to my bed, wraps me in a quilt and lays next to me stroking my hair gently.

'Sleep my darling, dream sweet dreams, you are my reason for living.' He continues stroking my hair.

My eyes grow ever heavier, 'I love you.' I manage to mutter.

Gabriel whispers softly, 'I love you too my sweet.'

Chapter 25 - Christmas and New Year festivities, oh what a drama!

Bouncing onto the sofa, I sit there and admire my work; All the Christmas decorations are up in both houses and are in line, no tilting, not one was out of place.

On my way home from work, I pick up the food that is required.

Everyone seemed excited over the past few days, well now it is Christmas eve, I knew I was running myself ragged but decided to clean my house and clean the Hanson household too.

Skipping back to my own house, it is time to feed on good old stew.

An hour passes, so I return to the Hanson household, the house feels lonely and empty without the usual chaos of the family.

7:00pm, everything done, time to relax and listen to some Christmas music, help me get into the spirit of the festive season.

All of a sudden, I feel I'm burning up, sticking a thermometer in my mouth, I wait impatiently for the result.

'No way,' I exclaim, looking at the thermometer, it reads forty-seven degrees Celsius 'this has to be a bad dream.'

Pinching myself, it is not a dream.

Feeling weak, dizzy and tired, I clear my head enough, so I can crawl upstairs and lay down on my bed.

The second flight of stairs; I feel worse than ever, only one more flight of stairs to go, putting my back against the cold wall I breathe a sigh of relief.

Tears come streaming down my face as I reach the top floor, 'Please let this fever die down for tomorrow.' I pray.

Flopping down on the large cold bed, I wrap myself up and close my eyes.

I'm being ripped apart, into separate components - my human self, the Phoenix and the Dragon, 'What the hell is going on?' I cry out.

The Phoenix is first to reply, 'I am the last of my kind, I am a third of you.' He bows his head.

'I am also the last of my kind,' booms the dragons voice, 'I am Dracona and I make up a third of you,' she growls, 'we cannot work together, one of us must go.'

Sitting down and sighing, 'There has to be a way, my human form can't tolerate this intrusion much longer.'

Standing up, I pace what I assume must be a floor, Dracona and the Phoenix follow on behind me, each of us in silence, each of us lost in thought.

With no warning, I grab both the Phoenix and Dracona, pushing them together, my body molds into theirs, as we melt into one, the human part of me is separate, but on looking over my shoulder, the Phoenix is nowhere to be seen, instead there is a red dragon, twice the size she was before.

'What the-' Are the words that leave my lips.

'You did it,' the red dragon calls, 'we have combined, now we are the Dranix, more powerful than we could ever have been on our own, thank you.' She smiles.

My fingers curl around the body of the Dranix, sweeping each muscle, defined and strong, then everything clouds over and becomes dark.

I am aroused by a cold smooth hand on my forehead, my eyes open but I can't regulate my breathing. I shoot bolt upright.

'What's wrong?' Gabriel asks in a blind panic.

He was about to call Michael up, when I put my finger to his lips, my eyes are full of fright and confusion.

'Honey, calm down, you're safe, take a deep breath.' Concern taints his voice.

Could I really tell him what had happened? For a moment I lose my voice, after a deep breath, I begin, 'My temperature rocketed, I crawled into bed, then something weird happened.' Standing up I walk slowly to the bathroom and grab a glass of water, I drink it greedily.

'She's a star,' calls Alison from downstairs, 'everything has been done.'

'You're welcome.' I shout down.

I feel exhausted, laying on the bed, I snuggle up to Gabriel. His arm wraps round me and his lips find my cheek, 'I love you.' He whispers in my ear.

'Love you too.' I say sleepily.

My nostrils detect the smell of frying bacon and dogs breath? Surely that can't be right?

Opening my eyes, Daniel is breathing over my face, slapping him on the cheek, 'Brush your teeth, please and out of here, let me wake up.'

'Merry Christmas to you too.' He laughs as he gets off the bed.

'Wait,' I call, he turns around, 'seriously, is it Christmas day?'

Daniel nods his head and wanders out, Gabriel sweeps in, a smile upon his face.

'Merry Christmas my sweet.' Gabriel says as he hands me a wrapped box.

I shuffle up the bed and take the box, 'Thanks,' I point under the bed, 'a little something for you.'

Carefully, I open the box, staring back at me is a large snowflake pendant, hanging on a delicate looking yet strong chain, the frosty sunlight highlights the red and blue stones that cover the structure of the snowflake.

'Are these,' shaking my head, 'I give up asking, those stones are rubies and sapphires.'

'You have more presents downstairs my love,' He smiles, 'I'll leave you alone for a bit,' He stands up.

'Wait, you haven't mentioned the little something I gave you.'

Gabriel swiftly opens the small package, inside is a poem written by me and a bracelet.

He kisses me passionately, 'They're perfect,' at the door, 'see you in a while.'

Gabriel leaves and I lay back against the bed smiling.

Christmas day went in the blink of an eye, everybody arrived on time, we laughed, we ate, opened presents, Michael bought me a tall original Tiffany lamp for my lounge, (I couldn't stop grinning), I observed Daniel and Anna for quite a bit of the day, something was going on.

By 8:00pm everyone had left, I settled and began reading a book. Michael, Callum and Alison were cleaning up, Gabriel sat next to me, his eyes not moving from me.

Within me, there was a storm brewing, something was waiting to go wrong, just a matter of time.

New Year's Eve, they've planned to do a family thing, before hunting on New Year's Day.

Why couldn't we sleep? Oh yeah, that's right, it is only me that requires sleep.

Because I've spent a few years alone, I have a set routine for New Year's Eve, that has been blown out of the window.

Anna and Daniel were due to come over after dinner; to play a few card games and maybe go for a midnight walk, could I really stand being in the same room as her for that long? I guess there's no other choice.

Sitting on the steps, I hear Anna's car coming down the lane, 'Bang goes my sanity.' I breathe.

Neither I nor Anna say a word to each other, instead she calmly walks by, ignoring my existence and into the house, I roll my eyes and take a deep breath.

Five minutes later, I am sat at the kitchen table, staring at Anna, the cogs of my mind keep turning, trying to find out if something is going on, or if it was my imagination.

'What the heck are you staring at? You foreigner.' Anna stares at me, waiting for an answer.

'I have no idea, but whatever it is, has a huge mouth for such a tiny animal.' I smile back.

Infuriated she replies, 'What does anyone see in you?'

Instead of answering, I give her the bird, smile and walk outside. I take a deep breath, 'Today will not end well.'

Something from deep within had worked out what was going on between Anna and Daniel, although it was none of my business, I storm inside, stand toe to toe with Anna and point my finger directly at her, 'You and Daniel are an item.' I scowl.

She smiles at me, just as she pins me to the wall, 'So what, got nothing to do with you, you don't own anyone.' She growls back.

'Neither do you, but you walk around here like you own the entire state, you give me the proof of otherwise and I'll be a slave.' Shoving her harshly, I wander into the kitchen.

The next ten minutes are a blur, the only things I remember are: a knife blade, blood, a bandage on my hand and someone using me as a speech vessel, I think that was Dracona, trying to get her point across.

Morning dawns, everyone is off on a hunt, I decide to stay home and take my Christmas decorations down.

'Are you sure honey?' Gabriel asks.

'Yep, Happy New Year my dear.'

'And to you too my love,' kissing my forehead, 'see you in two days.'

Anna brushes past me without a word, but she does put what's left of a molten knife into the trash bin, she takes one look at me as she gets into her car.

I have other ideas and walk into my home, hoping this year will be better than the end of the year just gone.

Chapter 26 - **First blood**.

It is close to the end of January, time seems to have passed me by at the speed of light.

I'm at work early, to catch up on paperwork before my first appointment arrives.

My mind is wandering a bit, mainly about a box Gabriel had hidden from me as I walked into the room on Christmas morning, 'Suppose it shouldn't really matter, must have been for someone else.' I speak aloud to the empty room.

Peeking out of the window, snow is falling heavily, making the landscape look isolated, an almost haunting quality to it.

Something new begins to haunt my mind, just when I could do without it.

Pushing it to the back of my mind, I try concentrating on the flakes of snow falling from a leaden sky.

Michael breezes in with a steaming hot coffee, 'Thought I'd drop this off,' he hands me the coffee, 'is something wrong?'

Michael sits in the chair opposite me, taking a deep breath, I don't know what to say, shrugging my shoulders, 'Nothing much, a niggle, you know? Like when you forget something but can't remember what it is.' I sniff the coffee with delight.

He looks me right in the eyes, 'Dreams can be like that too, you wake up crying but can't remember why,' Michael stands up, 'patients tell me all the time,' he takes my hand in his, 'do you require a lift home after work?'

I kiss his cheek, 'Thanks but no thanks, the walk home usually clears my mind, it's therapeutic.' There is a question on the tip of my tongue.

'Anything else?' Michael enquires.

'What do I bring to the world?' There, I'd said it, without hesitation.

Silence fills the air, making me feel nervous. Seconds pass like hours.

Michael puts his arm around my shoulder and rests his head upon my head, 'You my dear, bring light where there is dark, clarity where there is confusion and you break down barriers, even those that are centuries old,' he kisses my cheek, 'I know you do not believe me, you must see for yourself, one day you will see I am right.'

Shrugging my shoulders, 'Maybe.'

Michael smiles, 'You will, anyway Lydia, I shall be going, see you at home.' With that he walks out.

Time seems to drag, and I am thankful it is dinnertime.

I'm eating my dinner outside on the porch, watching more snowflakes fall from the leaden sky; my breathing begins to become shallow, out of the thick stream of snow, someone appears, taking a breath in, I take control of my breathing.

The male is my height, stocky build, spiky deep brown hair and almost bizarre green eyes, instinct tells me something isn't right about him.

He stares at me intently, 'Hi.'

I say nothing, instead I stare back at him.

'You're Michael's niece Lydia,' slight pause, 'he sent me to check up on you, to make sure you're okay,' he extends his hand, 'I'm Bruno.' He flashes a perfect grin.

His story doesn't add up, but for now I'm going along with it, 'That's me,' taking a sip of coffee, I shake his hand with my free hand, 'nice to meet you.' I feel like someone is bashing my head with a hammer, 'If you'll excuse me, I have to go now, getting a headache, tell Michael,' deep breath, 'I'm okay and I'll see him back home.'

Bruno smiles and I duck back inside and head for my office, not daring to look back.

It is 5:00pm, I am more than ready for my walk home, it may sort out some of the cobwebs and cloudiness in my mind, after saying goodbye to all the staff, I wrap my scarf around my neck, put on my winter hat and head out into the snowstorm.

Snow whips up around my legs, that isn't what is bothering me, Bruno was the problem, I can't believe how much he knew. My conclusion was; he had to be a vampire, working for whoever was out to eliminate me.

As I pass Mount Washington, I have a feeling that I'm being followed, looking around I can't detect who, even when I sniff the air, all I get is the night air, smoke from not too far away and crisp fresh snow. I don't feel happy about turning my back, there again on open ground I will always have my back towards something, 'This isn't funny.' I point to the ground before heading home.

Over the next few days, my routine is the same and whoever it is, still follows me.

Sitting at my desk, it's Friday afternoon, I know what I must do.

As the afternoon marches on, a plan forms in my mind, whether it will work or not, I have no idea.

'Time to go home.' I smile, on my way out, I wave to my work colleagues and head out of the door.

Two-hundred yards further down, there's a little café, I call in to have soup and a coffee.

An hour later; I'm fuelled up, ready to make my way home.

The streets are quiet and a mile further on, I have a choice to make - keep to the road or the open fields. With my mind made up I turn left into the open fields. The snow is almost a foot high, I don't care as I'm warm and well fed.

Half a mile in, the snow is coming down heavier, it is getting to a point where I can't see anything in front of me, or behind, I know my way home, despite not being able to see clearly.

There is a break in the relentless snow, to my left are the woods, so turning left I head in that direction.

Smelling the air, something isn't right, there's a distinct aftershave scent drifting close by, the wind riles the snow into my eyes, I feel almost blind, a hand clasps around my throat, pins me to a tree trunk with such force, the tree groans, again the snow dissipates. 'You.' I croak.

Bruno's husky voice replies, 'You smel good, I mean good.'

He unbuttons my coat, looks at my chest and continues his rant, 'They are voluptuous, the perfect shape,'

His free hand cups one and gently slides his thumb around it, I squirm at his touch, 'Leave me alone you creep.' I choke out.

Bruno tuts, 'After all the compliments I have given you,' he smiles widely as he brushes my thigh, 'so muscular, seems like you were made to be the perfect warrior,' he growls, 'definitely my type.'

'Tell me one thing,' I hesitate, 'before you murder me.' I grin weakly, my head is spinning.

Bruno nods his head.

'Why me? What part do I play in all this?'

Although it sounded like two questions, they were linked as one.

Bruno lets go of my throat, I slump to the floor.

He towers over me, 'You are the major part of what is to come, in order for it to go my masters way, you have to die,' he sighs, 'shame really, you'd be perfect for me,' Bruno bends down, 'the coming war will eat the Earth alive, before two winters pass, it will be here and vampires will rule.'

Without having to fully change, I feel fire pulsing through my veins, she has no need to appear.

Pushing with all my might, I send Bruno flying across the field. Running towards him, I feel I'm changing, I need some fire power.

His eyes reflect fear and hatred, before he has time to run, his body is shredded and set alight.

The smoke enters my nostrils, making me feel sick, quickly changing back, I run back to the woods, grab my bag and pull out my extra set of clothes, feeling my neck, it is tender and probably red.

Time to make my way home, new knowledge fresh in my mind.

Soon as I step into the house, I am swamped by Gabriel, he growls, 'What the hell happened?' He mutters through gritted teeth.

It would be nice if he asked if I was okay first, before launching into wanting details.

I slowly take the scarf from around my neck and point, 'A little incident.' My voice is gruff, and my throat is sore.

Gabriel embraces me, his hands rub gently up and down my back, 'I'm sorry,' he whispers, 'are you okay?'

'I'll be fine,' kissing his cheek, 'off to get a drink, be right back.' With that I wander off and out of the door.

Less than five minutes later and I walk back into the Hanson household, Gabriel is staring at me, I'm not sure what expression is crossing his face.

I decide to smile, 'I took care of him.'

'That doesn't stop the fact I want to protect you, I want to keep you safe, locked in my embrace forever.' Gabriel's voice is full of reverence.

His arm curls around my hip, I lean into him. So that was the expression crossing his face - the desire to protect me, he was concerned.

'I would love to stay wrapped in your arms forever, but I can't,' deep breath, 'I'm here for a reason and you can't protect me from everything.'

Gabriel looks me in the eye, he looks hurt and angry, 'You are my life, someone needs to look out for you, as you are looking out for everyone else.'

I guess he has a valid point, 'But this is the twenty-first century, so much has changed in over three-hundred years, it is amazing at how far man has developed.'

He sighs and pulls me in for a kiss, one thing is for sure - he knows how to melt me like butter.

A little while later, sitting around the dining table, some people are getting frustrated, there's no need for details, 'I took care of him,' Gabriel grabs my hand under the table.

Time to try a different tactic, 'before I finished him, he let slip information,' blank faces stare at me, 'don't you know what this means?' Still blank faces, 'he said, and I quote - "You are the major part of what is to come, in order for it to go my masters way, you have to die, the coming war will eat the entire Earth alive, before two winters pass, it will be here, and vampires will rule." '

Some sort of realisation crosses their faces, at last.

Smiling, 'We have time to prepare, this gives us an advantage,' opening the door and lighting up a cigarette, 'we need a plan, the sooner the better, I need to be prepared.' I look at Callum.

Gabriel tries to interrupt, I put my finger to his lips, 'The entire fate of the world rests on my shoulders, I need to be prepared.'

Chapter 27 - **Valentine's day**.

It is Friday 13th of February, the boys are doing my head in, being secretive and avoiding most of the questions Anna and I fire at them.

All we know is – they are taking us to New York later today.

Alison, Callum and Michael have already gone to New York, something about seeing a play they haven't seen in fifty years.

Anna and I are sat on the sofa watching a movie, I feel like I am falling asleep.

Daniel plods in, 'Pack your bags girls, we leave in an hour.' With that he plods back out with a grin on his face.

I look at Anna, she looks at me and shrugs her shoulders, 'Beats me.'

Gabriel walks in, grabs my hand and leads me outside, he pulls me in close, 'Go get your bag packed,' His husky voice echoes in my ear, sending a subtle buzz down my spine, 'I'll be there in five.' He nibbles my ear, sending my legs wobbling.

'Okay.' My voice stutters, with slightly wobbly legs I waddle into my home, into my bedroom and find a small suitcase.

Within sixty minutes we are packed and ready for the road trip. Anna insists she drive her car with Daniel and we follow on behind, 'Yeah sure,' I sigh, secretly breathing a sigh of relief, maybe Anna had the same thought?

Into the cars we get and leave the house behind.

For a change I'm driving, music is on full blast, looking over to Gabriel, I smile and carry on singing.

'It is amazing you were not already taken when I came into your life.' He rubs my hand, I turn the music down a little.

'No-one suited me, I was too far down the well of despair to even see daylight,' lighting a cigarette, 'you caught my eye and spoke to my heart.'

Gabriel smiles and begins rubbing my thigh, accidently triggering memories of Bruno, I flinch and almost recoil, keeping my eyes on the road, I try to take control of my thoughts.

'Pull over.' Gabriel asks.

I pull over, Gabriel whips out his phone and quickly speaks with Daniel, 'Yes, we will catch up shortly.'

Shifting my gaze from the dashboard, I look straight at Gabriel.

'Honey,' He soothes, 'what is wrong?'

'He was a creep, my body meant nothing, it was a toy to him, even for those few seconds, it wasn't relevant, he touched me, he paid for it, end of.'

Gabriel lets out a blood curdling growl, I rev the engine and pull back onto the road, New York here we come.

In the hotel room, (which is huge) I'm lounging on a massive sofa listening to music and drinking soda.

Anna knocks and walks in, 'Hey.'

'Hi.' I reply, turning the music up a little louder.

Anna shoves a beer in my hand and jumps onto the sofa, 'Drink that, you won't be as tense.' She smiles.

Opening the beer, I take a swig, foam comes streaming out of my nose, 'Damn it,' I laugh and guzzle the rest of the beer, 'What do you think they have in store for us?' I grab a tissue and blow my nose.

'Romantic meal, I guess,' takes a swig of her beer, 'we best get showered and changed,' at the door, 'see you soon.'

Okay, that was slightly strange, she gave me a beer and was being polite, have I missed something? 'Who knows.' I shrug, walk into the bathroom, undress and jump in the shower.

Walking out of the hotel room, Anna is just ahead of me, she stops and waits.

'Wow,' I stare at her, 'I'm lost for words.' The midnight blue backless dress frames her body, as if it was designed just for her, on one side there is a silver stripe.

'Thank you,' She bows, lifts her head and gives me the once over, 'You look so different with a dress on, I really like your look Lydia.'

I give myself the once over, a red silk knee length dress with spaghetti straps, a silk belt and a diamond encrusted snowflake to finish the outfit.

We link arms, into the lift to the ground floor. Walking out of the lift people are staring, mainly at Anna, she seems oblivious, looking to my left, a few people are staring at me, I smile and head for the door.

Standing by two sports cars are Gabriel and Daniel.

'Holy shit.' I think.

Both men look amazing in their tailored suits.

'I don't look good, not next to these three, I never will.' I try to smile.

Anna sighs happily as she embraces Daniel.

'You look like an angel.' Gabriel's voice is full of pride.

My face starts going red, I kiss him on the lips and climb into the car.

'Where we headed?' I ask timidly.

'Newark,' Gabriel smiles, 'not far from here.'

The engine roars to life, I hear the other cars engine come to life, pulling out into traffic, we're on our way to wherever the boys planned on taking us.

A waitress leads us over to a table for four, sitting down, I feel uncomfortable, but try not to show it, leaning over to Gabriel, 'I'm not comfy in this environment, people are staring.'
Yeah at Daniel, Gabriel and Anna, it made no sense that they would be staring at me.

'Tonight, we've made extra special, relax and enjoy it honey, remember, I love you.' He kisses my ear.

Later on, we are dancing, we're the only two couples dancing, I feel more at ease, thanks to Anna, who threw a few shots down my throat in the bathroom, before downing a few herself.

Resting my head against his chest, we gently sway to the music, 'What did I do to deserve you?' I question.

Gabriel cups my cheeks and brushes his lips against mine, 'I am nothing, you my sweetheart are worth everything.'

Daniel and Gabriel look at each other and nod, something is going on.

I watch as Daniel spins Anna around, as she comes to a halt, he gets down on one knee, smiling, a tear of happiness rolls down my cheek, I'm happy for them.

'Anna, will you marry me?' With that he opens a box, containing a gorgeous ring, a ring of such beauty, it must be one of a kind.

Anna gets down on both knees and kisses him, 'Yes I will.'

Daniel puts the ring on her finger, she beams proudly and gives me a quick flash of the ring, I smile happily back at her.

Looking across the room I see, Michael, Callum and Alison, so this was the plan, smiling I mouth 'Wow.' and beam.

'I love you, more than you will ever know,' Gabriel gets down on one knee and opens a green velvet box, 'Lydia, will you make me the happiest man alive by marrying me?'

My eyes dart to the ring, shock sets in. The ring has three pearls flanked by two rows of diamonds, it is amazing, looking round the entire room with teary eyes, I reply, my voice almost a whisper, 'I.' my emotions are choking my voice, 'I will Gabriel, yes.'

As Gabriel slips the ring on my finger, my family come over clapping and congratulating us all.

Two days since the proposal, I'm still in shock and awe.

Michael and Alison have arranged a party to celebrate the double engagement, it's a double-edged sword, but I'll get over it, eventually.

'What are you thinking about?' Gabriel asks.

'The engagement party, I don't know if to sing with joy, or hide like a rabbit.' I chuckle nervously.

'People care about you, that is the way they express their joy, excitement and maybe love.'

'I guess I never was one for the limelight, it was always for others.'

Gabriel puts his arm over me as we lay in bed, 'This time, you have to share the limelight, is that good enough for you?' He kisses my shoulder.

'Actually, that helps, least I'm not alone in the limelight.' I smile and kiss his hand.

I'm getting ready for a long walk, I need to try get the feel for the weather and its patterns. Stepping out of the door I tell the others, 'Catch me when you're ready.'

The wind is bitter, and the sky is grey. Being out in the vast expanse of land is invigorating.

Soon, I reach the woods, they'll know which way I've gone, it's easy, they follow my scent.

Half an hour later, I'm still on my own, no worries, I prefer to be on my own, sometimes.

Instinct is telling me something isn't right, I stand still, smelling the air and try to listen out for footsteps, 'Nothing,' I shrug my shoulders and continue on my journey.

Seven miles further, I stop and take a break.

At first it didn't occur to me, after a moment I notice the wildlife is silent, not a bird tweets or creature scuttles, 'This can't be good.'

Putting my backpack down and wait for whatever is coming.

To my right, something moves quickly, darting in and out of the trees.

'Okay, ha ha,' I moan, 'show yourself, there's only me here.'

From the East, six figures emerge slowly from the trees, shaking slightly I know that if I have to fight, this will not be easy. I maybe immortal but that doesn't stop me from being scared.

'We've being looking for you.' The girl with the black necklace says.

'Well, that was a waste of time,' I sneer, 'I'm not in the mood for trouble.'

'You are the one that can destroy us all.' Her voice is menacing.

'Well, I kinda guessed that part,' I laugh, 'are you here to waste my time?'

The girl growls, I stand there pretending to shake with fear.

From behind me come - Michael, Callum, Alison and Gabriel.

'Phew.' Sighing with relief.

The girl and the rest of them begin to back up, 'Some other time.' She taunts.

'Yeah, remember to give me a ring first.' I fling back.

Again, she growls, I take a few steps forward, I begin to change, her eyes show outrage and fear, they all disappear within seconds.

Stepping back, I flex and return to normal, 'Come on,' I yell, 'more sights to be seen.'

Chapter 28 - **An engagement party**.

Already mid-March, tomorrow is the engagement party.

Callum said it had to be a costume party, 'Why?' I ask.

'Makes it more interesting.' He grins back.

'Fine,' I huff, 'dammit.'

Sticking my head in the wardrobe, I can't see anything I want to wear, that is until I spy a box stuck in the corner, 'God sake.' Yelling at the wardrobe.

Sitting on my bed, I open the box, inside is what appears to be a 1920's dress. Carefully bringing it out, I stare in utter amazement, the dress is a white silk under-dress with an intricate gold lace outer and gold tassels framing the hem. Looking in the box, there are white silk gloves, a pearl necklace and a pair of jazzy black and white high heeled bar shoes.

Rushing into the bathroom, I try on the dress, beaming I walk out of the bathroom, 'That's what I'm wearing tomorrow.'

Tea-time, this time a noodle medley quickly thrown together, I want a long hot soak with candles and music.

Someone knocking on the bathroom door rouses me from daydreaming, 'Come in.' I call.

Gabriel comes in and sits down on the floor next to the bath, 'How are you love?'

'Tired.'

The flickering of the candles seems to highlight Gabriel's facial features, I helplessly stare at him.

Lips brush against mine, automatically my lips respond but my eyes stay glued to him.

Whispering in my ear, 'Love, is something wrong?'

I land back in reality with a bump, flickering my eyes, 'The candlelight frames your features, I was melting.' My voice distant.

Gabriel laughs huskily, 'Well, melt some other time,' He kisses my shoulder followed by my collar bone, 'yum,' He grins wickedly, 'I will see you later, at the party, Alison will be with you soon.'

My face falls, I can't believe he's going, leaving me all hot and flustered, 'Bye.' I say quickly, I've half a mind to pull him into the bath with me.

Touching 7:00pm, on cue Alison walks in, 'I'm here to do your hair and make-up, I-' she stammers, lost for words.

'Something wrong?' I turn to face her, it is as if someone has pressed pause on the TV remote, 'Hello, anybody home?' I wave a hand in front of her.

'Lydia,' She gasps, 'you look stunning, truly you do,' smiling, 'I know exactly what make-up and hairstyle to do, they're all going to be shocked.'

Turning bright red, 'I doubt that.'

'We'll see.' Alison smiles.

As we walk into the Hanson house, I can hardly believe my eyes, 'This is fantastic,' I scream in delight, 'I shall remember tonight for the rest of my life.'

Alison beams, 'Thank you,' whispers, 'Neither Gabriel or Daniel will recognise you.' With that she leaves me standing by the bar, I pour myself a Malibu and coke, waiting for the others to turn up.

I don't have to wait long, the room begins to fill up, Anna walks straight up to the bar and pours herself a drink, 'Hi,' She says to me, confusion crosses her face, Anna takes another look, 'Bloody hell Lyd, I didn't know it was you.'

I can't reply straight away, swallowing I can manage one word, 'Thanks.'

Refilling my glass, I clink glasses with Anna, 'Cheers.' We both say.

Daniel is dancing with Anna, as Gabriel walks in, his eyes dart from person to person trying to spot me, I'm in a corner happily drinking coke, his eyes brush over me and then away, Alison points me out and I raise my glass. In a heartbeat he is at my side, his eyes look me up and down several times, hunger and lust flash in his eyes.

'Good evening Mr. Hanson.' I smile, trying to hide my face.

Pinning me to the wall, Gabriel kisses my neck, 'You're the image of perfection,' kisses the other side of my neck, 'If it wasn't for all these guests, I would ravage you here and now.'

I raise my eyebrows, 'Maybe later.' I wink and wander off, leaving Gabriel standing there.

After the food, announcements and introductions, it was time to go onto the dance floor.

Looking at Gabriel I sigh, 'I love you.'

Gabriel pulls me in closer, 'And I love you sweetheart, more than you will ever know.'

Daniel begins to dance like no-one is watching, Anna is blushing slightly, and I join in, trying to do the Charleston, with hilarious results.

Midnight comes and goes, the party begins to wind down, Anna and Daniel say their goodbyes and head to Anna's place, as for Gabriel and I, we wish everyone goodnight, we thank Alison, Michael and Callum for all their efforts and head home.

I don't have the energy to go upstairs to bed, I lay on the couch with a blanket, resting on Gabriel's legs, he leans in for a kiss. The kiss is red hot, full of desire and passion.

One vampire fascinates me, his name is Samuel and is over two-hundred and twenty-seven years old, with dark brown hair and soft sea blue eyes.

Sunday afternoon, everyone is out, they left me sleeping peacefully.

Walking into the Hanson house, Sam gives me a fright, 'Jeez Sam,' holding onto the wall, 'I nearly slapped you.'

'I am sorry my dear Lydia,' hand gesture, 'please, make yourself a drink.'

In the kitchen, I can feel his eyes watch my every move.

'So, Lydia,' He sits on the sofa and pats it, 'come sit down, I won't bite,' smiling innocently, 'tell me about yourself.'

I sit at the far end of the sofa, 'There isn't much to tell, I'm immortal, I love reading, history and above all I'm engaged to Gabriel, the sweetest, sexiest vampire I know.'

There is a hint of anger in his reply, 'He is the only vampire you know.'

I shake my head, 'Out of all the ones I have met, he is right for me.'

Out of impulse Sam replies, 'You are stunning.'

Oh gawd, please tell me he isn't hitting on me? 'Gabriel tells me all the time, I'm still getting used to it.'

He mumbles, 'He will tell anyone that.'

Sam looks as if he is foaming at the mouth, I haven't time for this drama.

'Let me guess - Gabriel used to date Anna and it didn't work out,' I breathe, 'I don't care if he dated Marilyn Monroe,' growling, 'you sound jealous.' I give him a smug look.

The front door goes, Sam puts his arm around me, just as Gabriel walks in, I can no longer bottle up my anger, taking his arm, I place back on Sam's lap and punch him before walking out.

Storming back into my home, I grab a can of soda, walk back out, growl as Sam walks out of the house and storm off towards Mount Washington, I need the air, to breathe, before I make a mistake.

A pair of cool hands wrap around my waist, spinning round it is Gabriel, relief floods my body, 'Hello.' I sigh.

'Anything wrong?'

'Yes,' I snort, 'Sam is getting under my skin,' realising, 'did you not see his arm around me when you walked in?'

Gabriel begins growling, 'I can't believe he upset you, what did he say?'

'Gabe, he's jealous of you, he tried it on with me,' I place my finger on his lip, 'that's why I punched him, I will keep my eye on him.' I smile.

'So, will I.' Gabriel chunters, 'so will I.'

Chapter 29 - **Practice, losing my temper**.

Taking a week off work, purely to practice, nine hours and counting, until practice begins.

Callum has never told me much about himself, only that he'd met Alison ninety years ago, before that he was on his own.

Just before 11:00pm, stretching, I crawl out of bed and jump in the shower.

With the stereo on full blast, I waltz into the kitchen and make some supper and a brew.

1.30am, on the field doing stretching exercises, sniffing the air, Sam is approaching, 'Wonderful.' I mumble.

Sam stands beside me and smiles, 'Good evening.'

'Yeah.' I sigh, pretending he isn't really there, until he rubs my leg.

Standing bolt upright, I stare hard at him, 'Do not do that ever again.' I poke him hard in the chest.

Grinning he wriggles his fingers at me, I growl and move away.

Gabriel kisses the back of my neck, 'You're early.'

Bending down, I place my head in my hands, 'Wish I hadn't,' looking up at Gabriel, 'he violated my personal space by,' taking a deep breath, 'rubbing my leg.'

Ah shit, shouldn't have told him, before I can react, Gabriel has Sam pinned against a tree, 'You leave her the hell alone, don't ever,' growling, 'come near her again.' Gabriel walks back to me and kisses my hand.

Yep, I'm partnered with Sam, Gabriel is not happy, he comes up to me, 'Will you be okay with him?' He looks across at Sam with venom in his eyes.

'I should be, but if he starts anything, I'll kill him.' I sigh and go over to Sam.

Let practice commence.

Early on Thursday, Anna sits next to me, 'Hi.'

'Morning.' Itching my arm.

'Some advice,' She whispers, 'Sam is dangerous, he's never come across anyone like you and will stop at nothing to get what he wants.' Anna nudges me.

'I'm not a trophy, Sam knows that.' Frustration clear in my voice.

'That won't stop him.' Anna sighs.

Helping me up, we wander inside, you can cut the tension with a knife.

2:00am fast approaches, I'm getting ready for more practice, Gabriel is being protective of me, 'Gabe, I can look after myself ya know.'

'Sam isn't the type to give up, you don't know him like I do,' wrapping his arms around my waist, 'he doesn't see you like a person, he sees you as a trophy,' kissing my cheek, 'Sam may hurt you and I will not allow it.'

I knew Gabriel meant well, what scared me, was the fact that Sam might hurt me.

Daniel runs across the field, picks me up and spins me around, 'Lyd, I've missed you loads.'

He puts me down, my head is spinning, 'I love ya too.' I grin.

Hand in hand with Daniel and Gabe, we go join the others.

Callum takes Daniel and a few other shape shifters to one side, to show them how to deal with new born vampires.

Callum partners me off with Sam, neither Daniel or Gabriel seem happy.

Gabriel walks over and has angry words with Callum, I'm not having Callum dragged into this, I walk over.

'Gabe, leave it, I'll be fine, if not I know what to do.' I kiss his cheek and walk over towards Sam, 'Don't think I'm soft, in fact I'm betting you were a spoilt brat growing up.' The words just came out.

Sam leans in and whispers, 'You will be mine.'

Yawning, I ignore his threat, 'Let's just do this.' I growl back.

As I launch myself at Sam, he grabs me by the throat, puts me on his back and runs.

'What the hell? I yell.

Sam snarls back, 'If I can't have you, it is time for drastic action.'

Looking backwards, Gabriel is about to launch himself at Sam, I'm in the way, Daniel is snarling and is a split second behind Gabe.

'Ah shit.' I groan, as my body is launched into the air, Daniel is howling and leaves his spot next to Gabe, to run after my falling body, instead of feeling the grass, I feel fur, quickly getting up I hope Daniel is okay? 'Daniel, you okay?' I kneel down and rub between his ears.

A homely sound emanates from his chest, like a cat purring, he turns over and licks my face.

Despite the growling and arguing, I kiss Daniels ear and wander away, my mind racing with panic.

Three weeks later, I look a mess, I've hardly slept, when I do manage to sleep I have nightmares about Sam hurting me and leaving me for dead. More time off work, I can hardly focus.

Everyone is off hunting, I need a hug, but that isn't gonna happen, needing to clear my head, I grab my coat and head out for a walk.

This morning, Daniel had said if I felt threatened by Sam, I was to tell him, but he and Anna are happy, the last thing they need is me running to them for comfort.

The early spring air fills my lungs, it's twilight outside.

Hackles on the back of my neck rise, something doesn't feel right, taking a look around, no-one is in sight, smelling the air there are no new scents.

Rubbing my temples, I tell myself that I'm imagining things and to carry on with my walk.

Leaning against a tree is Sam's silhouette, I have a bad feeling about this, 'Hi Sam.' I call.

Sam looks me in the eye, 'Hi.'

'Have you been following me?' I ask quietly.

He sighs heavily.

Crossing my arms, I'm angry and spooked out, 'This is the final time I'm gonna tell you, I'm not a trophy.'

Fire flashes in his eyes and fragments of my nightmare are starting to slot into place.

I knew all about his gift and that was scarier than any nightmare my mind could produce.

Sam gets into crouch position, in a flash he sends me flying, he catches me mid-air and slams me hard on the ground, 'If I cannot have you, no-one will.' He growls.

I'm too busy trying to catch my breath to reply, pain seared through me.

Blood was oozing from my head, trying to stand up was impossible, I fell straight back to the ground.

Sam drags me up by the chin, my feet can't touch the floor, for a second, he is distracted by the blood dripping from my head, this would be my chance, I am too slow to react.

He licks the blood running down my neck and looks into my eyes. Despite the pain I am in I'm determined to get him off me and make a run for it.

I call on what strength I had left in me, to change, Sam is blocking my ability, spitting in his eye, it gives me the chance, bursting into flames, I knock Sam to the floor and slump to the ground, swiftly I start crawling, Sam runs off in the opposite direction.

I hadn't got far, after an hour of crawling, my entire body is protesting, all I can do now is lay here.

Weakly, I shout, 'Sam,' breathing, 'you either help me or finish me, you hear me?' I yell, 'Make the choice.'

Twenty minutes later and Sam's outline appears, his head hung low.

'Sam,' I'm out of breath, 'have you made your choice?'

He falls to his knees, 'I saw into your soul, deeper than I had ever seen, you were right, it's not about trophies,' He sighs, 'it's about the choices we make.'

Finally, he had realised what I'd been trying to tell him.

Sam grabs my hand and helps me up, I lean on him for support, 'I also saw that you truly love Gabriel,' Sam smiles weakly, 'I hope to find my mate someday.'

'I'm sure you will Sam, when you least expect it.' Offering a small smile.

'I am truly sorry for all the trouble I have caused,' we stop for a moment, 'I promise to help you win this war.'

He wraps his arms around me, scoops me up and runs towards home.

I am left leaning on my porch for support as Sam walks slowly towards the Hanson house.

'Sam?' I call out.

'Yes?' Turning around to face me.

'Let me explain it to them.'

'It has to come from me.' Sam lowers his head.

He turns and walks in. Growls and hisses come from the house, then silence falls.

My heart rate speeds up.

Gabriel comes storming out of the house, soon as he sees me, he races over and scoops me up, 'Sweetheart,' He kisses me several times, 'are you hurt?'

'Nothing that a few days rest won't cure,' I whisper, 'don't be hard on Sam, it has been a hard learning curve.'

Gabriel opens the door to our house, lifts me inside and shuts the door.

Chapter 30 - **Non-stop, second thoughts**.

We were all out on the field, it is 3:00am and I'm starting to fall asleep stood up. All week we had been practising, I haven't slept, Callum said I may have to fight sleep deprived.

Stephenie knocks me to the ground, I can't even wriggle in pain, my muscles are aching too much.

'Callum, she isn't a soldier.' Gabriel whispers.

'She has to become one, there is no way she can rest on her laurels when the time comes.' Callum replies sternly.

Gabriel hisses, 'Lydia is still a human, she needs a break.'

'We were all human once,' Callum takes Gabriel to one side, 'I know you're worried about her, but she needs this, it will be an advantage to her.' Callum rests his arm on Gabriel.

Growling I put both hands to my head, 'Fuck it.'

Sharp pains hit me from all sides, Gabriel and Callum rush to my side.

'Are you okay love?' Gabriel asks softly.

My eyes water, 'I think so, should pass soon,' looking at Callum, 'I know I need this, but I also need a break, just twenty-four hours, someone at work is covering for me, I keep getting angry in front of patients.'

Callum bends down, 'Okay, twenty-four hours rest, then straight on to it, you need to be prepared.' He pats my shoulder and wanders off.

Staggering about, I make it to my front door before collapsing, unable to move but still aware of everything going on around me.

I see Gabriel's arms reach and scoop me off the floor, 'Hey honey, you'll be okay, I promise.'

I smile goofily as my eyelids fall.

The heavenly scent of frying eggs alerts me and wakes me up with a grin.

Pottering downstairs, I'm surprised to see Callum preparing breakfast.

'Good morning Lydia.' He chirps as he serves me a brew.

'Morning.' I reply feeling a little puzzled.

'I'm sorry I am pushing you hard, do you understand why?' Flipping the eggs.

To be prepared?' I sip my brew.

'Precisely,' He sits down opposite me, 'I was born at a time when war was rife and being a man was when you were about eleven,' deep breath, 'soon I will tell you about my life before being a vampire.'

Callum strides over to the pan and serves up the eggs.

1:00am on the field, I'm feeling refreshed and ready for action.

Callum taps me on the shoulder, 'Just us tonight, no distractions.'

Rubbing my hands with glee, I grin from ear to ear, 'Let's do this.'

We practice until 7:00am, he shows me moves, I put them into action, sometimes we laugh, but we knew when the time came there'd be no laughing.

8:00am and the others return, we are practising and I am feeling stronger than ever, running backwards, I aim an arrow at Callum just how he showed me, it missed him, by an inch.

Another ten days pass by like minutes, I'm surviving on an hour's sleep, little food but keeping up the liquids. I don't feel any stronger, neither do I feel any weaker, maybe this training is working?

We would practice more over winter, when days are short, and the practice will be longer.

I'm proud of myself for not giving up and grateful to Callum for not giving up on me.

The travelling fair has arrived in Lancaster, time for a trip out.

Holding Gabriel's hand, we decide to walk the few miles, with the others following on behind.

Sunshine is beaming down and there is a brisk wind but that's alright, it makes the journey easier.

Callum catches up with me, I let go of Gabriel's hand and potter over.

'So, Lydia, do you have any interests?' Callum asks.

That's a question I wasn't expecting, 'Besides reading, history, cooking, fencing and swimming, I love watching ice hockey games and car racing like the Indy 500, the Daytona cup, always loved racing, might have to book a race day sometime in the future.'

'Never would have had you down for racing, or ice hockey for that matter.'

'I've spoken to people who race, and it gave me chills, gonna try my hand at it, just for fun.' I slap Callum on the back.

He looks at me all puzzled, until he works out why I slapped his back, by then I'm already half a mile away, laughing.

Walking into the fair, I feel normal, whatever normal is. A smile lights up my face and I head over to the dodgems.

The great and tempting smell of burgers wafts by my nose, I could no longer resist, jogging over to the burger stall, I order three burgers and a soda.

Soon as my teeth touch the meat, I feel like melting, this is something I hadn't had for a long while.

'Oooo, candy floss.' I grin.

A little boy, aged about five catches my eye, he looks upset and lost, walking over I bend down on my knees, 'Are you lost?' I ask him gently.

The little boy nods his head and proceeds to suck his thumb.

'When did you last see your mummy? Or daddy?' Surely, they wouldn't let him wander the fair alone?

He starts to cry, a soft whimpering sound, my eyes begin to fill, taking a deep breath, 'Awe, little man, I'm sure we can reunite you very soon, I promise.' I hand him a sweet. I rub his shoulder.

Standing up, I scan the crowds, no-one seems worried, looking at the boy, 'What's your name? My name is Lydia.'

He whispers in my ear, 'My name is Jason.'

'Pleased to meet you J-' Somewhere in the crowd and the noise, a woman's voice is calling out the name Jason, 'Jason, does your mummy have long red hair, green eyes and is about my height?'

Jason's smile lights up his face, waving my hand furiously, the woman sees me, then only has eyes for Jason, tears roll from her eyes and a smile that could light the world. She comes racing over to Jason, picks him up and hugs him tight. I couldn't be happier.

Jason whispers in his mum's ear, 'This is Lydia.'

She places him down and holds his hand, with the other hand she reaches out for me and hugs me, 'Thank you,' She whispers, 'thank you, I lost sight of him for a second and he was gone.'

'I'm glad I was able to help.' I am desperate to cry.

Mother and child hand in hand, they turn and begin to walk away, I wave to Jason, he waves back and just before they're out of sight, both of them turn and wave, Jason even blows me a kiss.

The tears overflowed, one little boy was no longer lost.

Turning around, I see Gabriel staring at me, 'Let's go.' I choke trying to get rid of tears sliding down my cheeks.

He puts his arm round my shoulder and kisses my forehead, 'That was simply amazing, you are amazing.'

Chills ran up and down my spine as I sit in the big wheel, something was strange about the recent news article, something huge had been spotted over the skies of Ireland, no-one could accurately describe it, only that it was huge, had wings and echoes of a roar could be heard like thunder.

Grabbing my mobile, I ring Morgan.

'Hello.' A voice says quietly.

'Hi, it's Lydia, just ringing to see how you're doing?'

'Meh,' Morgan replies dismissively.

'I was thinking of visiting you in September.' I hoped that would cheer him up.

'You can't,' He says quickly, 'found a job in New York, moving around August,' something seems to be distracting him, 'when I arrive, I'll arrange to meet, gotta go, bye.'

The line is dead, and I'm slightly pissed off at him for being evasive.

'Haven't the time for him, waste of my time.' I grumble to myself.

Eating dinner, it dawns on me – I don't want to do this, I wanted a life, not a half-life, someone else could be the saviour, this is something I no longer wish to see through to its conclusion.

Outside, Stephenie is enjoying the vista. Maybe I can ask her why I feel conflicted?

'Hi Lydia,' She steps aside and offers an open arm, 'something wrong?'

I curl an arm around her, she looks at me with concerned eyes.

'Let's take a walk.' I offer.

After a few miles, all is quiet, sighing loudly I sit on the ground.

'Are you having second thoughts?'

My eyes grow wide, how the hell did she know that? It's impossible, how could she know? I haven't breathed a word to anyone.

Confession time, 'I'm ready to run,' gulping, 'I'm scared of losing people I care about and I'm always asking, "Why me"?'

Stephenie looks at me, 'It is impossible to run away from your problems, they only follow you, this thing will catch up with you eventually, and by then will there won't be anyone left to fight for?'

I knew she was right, deep inside, I had known all along that I would never run, as whatever it was, would catch up on me sooner or later.

'When you get a sign, that is when you will make your decision, until then, breathe and enjoy each moment of freedom.'

'How will I know it's the sign?'

She points to my heart, 'That is where you will feel it, any other questions?'

'If I do win this war, yet everyone I care about is dead, what was the point in fighting?'

Somehow, I already knew the answer to that.

'The sacrifice of the few for the many, it is a price we must pay,' looks directly at me, 'I see it in Gabriel's eyes, if he loses you, he will never recover, the day he met you is the day you stole his heart.' Stephenie grins.

'No-one can expect more of me than what I give, which will be everything, yet I am nothing, just a leaf in the breeze.'

Replying sternly yet gently, 'If only you truly knew how much you mean to us all, you wouldn't say that, but until you believe it, my words are exactly that - just words, brush away the self-doubt and worry, one day you will be free, and you will worry no longer.'

'I hope so,' I mumble, 'truly, I hope what you say is true.'

Chapter 31 – The sign.

There's a connection between Daniel and I, though neither of us are sure what the connection is.

Opening the front door, to my amazement, Daniel is standing there with a goofy grin.

I try giving him a bear hug, as always, he wins, 'Missed you.' I smile.

Both of us sit on the porch.

'Missed ya too lugs.'

Lugs? Did he just give me a lame nickname? Wait til I get him back.

'So,' I open a beer, 'what you been up to since last we met?' I can see the confusion in his eyes, I rarely speak old style.

'Not much,' nudges me, 'beer please,' pulls the ring pull, 'though a few nights ago a vampire was on our land.'

I nearly choke on the beer in my mouth, too late, foamy beer streams out of my nose and I gasp for air, 'You sure?' I blurt out before coughing my guts up.

'Guess we had a weak moment, after we squeezed information out of him, we let him go,' serious voice, 'Lydia they know more than we thought, not only that, it seems they're itching to start it, but something or someone is stopping them.'

'They must be waiting for a signal from their commander.' although outside I seemed relaxed, inside I shook to the core with fear.

Daniel nods his head and stands up, 'Gonna get some shut eye,' helps me up, 'haven't had any sleep yet,' pulls me into him, 'fancy patrol tomorrow night? It's an all-nighter.'

I'm too busy mumbling, 'Next year, by then it's either win or lose.'

'Lydia,' He snaps his fingers, 'so,' pause, 'do you fancy pulling an all-nighter on patrol tomorrow?'

Smiling I reply, 'Yeah sure, sounds good,' feeling flustered and emotional, 'go on, get some sleep, see you tomorrow around 11:00pm.'

Daniel kisses my forehead, 'Sure you're gonna be okay?' He sounds deeply concerned.

'Yeah,' I sigh, 'just little niggles, nowt I can't handle.' Patting him on the back.

Running at top speed, wind rushing through my hair, the moon above me and the ground beneath my feet. We are almost there - something flickers before my eyes, slumping to the ground, I can hear Daniel howling.

I'm not there anymore, instead I find myself in a place I've seen before. It felt almost a thousand years ago, two children run by me, the girl teasing the boy.

'Sarah, Luke,' A voice calls, 'stop teasing your brother Sarah and help me clean up.'

Sarah looks about seven years old, with long blonde hair and crystal blue eyes.

I somehow know that Sarah is a past version of me.

Looking at Luke, he is maybe eleven years old with flame red hair and green eyes. He looks directly at me, in that moment Daniels face morphs into Luke's and then fades.

The scene changes to that of carnage, people screaming in agony, horses' rider less and just on the horizon, I see Sarah with her brother Luke, crawling along the ground, I reach the spot they are standing on.

Luke is crying, begging Sarah not to go through with it, Sarah however, is more composed, she kisses his forehead before running into battle, Luke's screams can be heard, it seems he is mourning the loss of his sister, before walking into the Earthly hell himself.

Panicked voices are bringing me back to the present.

Gabriel's voice crept over the others, 'Lydia, honey can you hear me?'

'Wow, wasn't expecting that.' My mind swims with what I had seen.

'What was strange love?' Gabriel asks as he kneels down.

'Seeing all that, to finally know the connection between Daniel and me.'

With my head spinning, I stand up and wobble over to Daniel, he stands up, crying he wraps his huge arms around me, 'Now we know the connection,' coughs and chokes on the last word, 'sister.'

This is the sign and connection Stephenie talked to me about, 'I now know my path brother.' I'm ready to burst into tears.

'No matter what, I will protect you,' Daniel furiously kisses my forehead, 'path?'

'Before tonight, I was confused about something, I've had the sign I need,' deep breath, 'we fight for what is right and-' a little smile, 'it will be I that protects you, the way it has always been.'

Held in our embrace, tears flow freely.

In twenty-four hours' time, the visiting vampires are leaving, watching them all, I see changes within them. Sam with his new outlook on life and finally to Stephenie, with whom I'd had many conversations with and have forged a bond with.

Make this last day be the best yet.

6:00am and we are heading for Vancouver, to do a bit of sightseeing before having dinner in the park.

The Sun beats down as we reach Vancouver, teeming with life and nature. I feel alive and at peace with the demons that lurk within.

In the park, Daniel and I were throwing a Frisbee, my body begins to heat up, finding the shade, I rest my body against the tree.

Rex disappeared, returning a few minutes later, 'Lydia, chew on these for a few minutes, they should do the trick.'

Putting my thumb up, I hold out my hand, grab the leaves and berries. Placing them in my mouth, I chew away, hoping they work.

An hour later and I'm feeling much better, Gabriel is sat with me, keeping me cool, 'You feeling better sweetheart?'

'Much better, not sure why that happened,' pause, 'but I'm ready to head home.'

'Well my love, I insist on carrying you home, I want to make sure you're safe.'

His voice is gentle, blushing I nod my head, 'I won't argue,' slight chuckle, 'for once.'

I feel safe on Gabriel's back, I feel like nothing on this Earth can hurt me here and as my heart pumps loudly against his back, the rush of the wind sends me gently off to sleep.

Sunrise the following morning, although as of yet I haven't been to bed, (we spent part of the night dancing under the stars, the rest of the night, we spent playing card games.) The visitors are ready to leave, in some ways I feel sad, but I knew they would be returning over the winter. We all exchanged numbers, so we can keep in contact. After many hugs, handshakes and farewells, they walked off into the distance.

Leaning on Gabriel, half asleep, he whispers in my ear, 'We have a surprise for you love.'

Managing to tilt my head I smile, 'Sounds good but right now sleep sounds better.'

June 12th, the day before my birthday. I wasn't feeling too excited, whereas the others were ready to make a fuss. Not long and we are heading to New York for two days, tomorrow they'd arranged for us all to see a Broadway show, if I'm honest, I'd rather have some alone time, shows, operas etc... aren't my style.

Daniel should be here in a minute, some quality time before heading down to New York.

Daniel and I had decided upon a picnic about a mile away from home. Geez he doesn't half pack food, you would think we were feeding thirty people.

'Dan, did you bring enough food?' My eyes scan the amount of food laid out.

'Yeah, mind you, I forgot the cheese.' He grins.

'Never mind the cheese,' pointing, 'there's enough here to feed half the world's population.'

Daniel gets comfy, whereas I'm stretching.

'You excited about your birthday?'

Blowing out air, 'Not really, just another day to me but everyone is insisting on celebrating it.' I feel flustered.

'I know you'd rather have alone time,' sighs, 'but we give a damn so just suck it up, you can have alone time some other time.'

Sitting down, I burst out laughing, when Daniel tries to be serious he sounds comical.

'Let's enjoy the moment.' I'm sniggering.

Sitting in the back of a limousine, family surrounding me, driving through New York to the show.

'Happy birthday gorgeous.' Gabriel says.

Shit, I'm blushing again, 'Thanks love.' I mumble before standing up and sticking my head out of the sun roof.

Tall buildings pass us, yellow cabs, horses, a huge park and of course people staring at a mad woman sticking her head out, the noise is almost deafening and disorientating.

Clambering down, I take my seat.

At which point, they all burst into singing Happy birthday.

Gabriel gently strokes my leg, 'Can't wait to get you back to the hotel room.' He plants a seductive kiss on my cheek, which automatically sends my mind spinning.

'You sure I look okay?'

When I look in a mirror, all I see is me, nothing else, I'm not as confident as I want to be.

Gabriel's eyes grow wide, 'Why do you ask such a question?'

'I don't see myself like others do, all I ever see is me.'

'One day, you will see yourself as I do, completely gorgeous, tempting and mind blowing.' Gabriel's voice is full of pride.

My cheeks glow a brighter red, just as the limo pulls up outside the theatre.

Despite the coolness of the theatre, the overwhelming heat being pumped by my body was starting to get to me. Sweat starts to roll down my forehead, turning to Gabe, 'Love, I have to go out and get some fresh air.' My heart is beating fast.

'Are you alright honey?' Gabriel grabs my hand and feels my forehead.

Shakily I get to my feet, 'Just ten minutes, I should be okay after that.' I give him a weak smile and blindly make my way outside.

Under the sky and air, my heart quickens, I'm in so much agony I want to scream out that, I feel like I'm dying.

Printed in Poland
by Amazon Fulfillment
Poland Sp. z o.o., Wrocław